CODE OF THE HILLS

A MICK HARDIN NOVEL

CODE OF THE HILLS

CHRIS OFFUTT

THORNDIKE PRESS
A part of Gale, a Cengage Company

LIBRARY OF CONGRESS CIP DATA ON FILE.
CATALOGUING IN PUBLICATION FOR THIS BOOK
IS AVAILABLE FROM THE LIBRARY OF CONGRESS.

ISBN-13: 979-8-88578-982-0 (hardcover alk. paper)

Published in 2023 by arrangement with Grove/Atlantic, Inc.

Printed in Mexico
Print Number: 1   Print Year: 2023

For James Offutt

I never met a Kentuckian who wasn't either thinking about going home or actually going home.

— Albert Benjamin "Happy" Chandler, former Governor of Kentucky

CHAPTER ONE

Janice drove slowly to avoid jostling the plastic containers of food on the floor behind her seat. She had better ones at home, but her father was likely to use them for storing nuts and bolts. She brought him food twice a week and resented it — the cooking, the drive, the awkward struggle for a topic other than weather or his cars. It was a matter of proximity. Janice was the oldest of his four adult kids and the only one who lived close. She often wished he'd died before her mother. With his wife gone he'd turned useless and low. Nothing engaged him but working on cars and taking care of his chickens.

At the turnoff for his holler, she tried to straddle the mud holes, an impossible task given their width. They were dry, which made her tires bounce harder. She had a choice with the last one — go through it at the rate of a drugged turtle, or crowd the edge and risk sliding through horseweed into the ditch. Janice never cursed out loud, but her mind flew with blue language. Eff it, she thought and pressed the accelerator, the old shocks scraping metal as the tires dropped into a four-inch hole.

The driveway piddled out into the hard-packed yard filled with five cars — three for parts, one he drove, and one he was working on. He hadn't been to a store in six months. She couldn't remember the last time he'd visited her. Maybe it was for the best, she thought. He smelled of sweat, cigarette smoke, and engine oil. His hands were black with grease embedded deep in the pores from decades of mechanical work.

She honked to let him know she was there, got out of the car, and opened the rear door. Sure enough, there was a pool of spaghetti sauce on the cardboard she'd placed beneath the containers. A second one had spilled lettuce onto the carpet, a salad she'd dutifully made, despite knowing he wouldn't eat it. The lid to the pasta had slid under the seat and she decided to get it later. He wouldn't care. He'd probably eat it with his fingers over the sink.

She carried the food onto the porch, pulled the screen door with a finger, kicked it open, and entered. The familiar smell of her mother's hand soap and lotion drifted under the thicker layer of a man alone. The twined scents always reminded her of better days in the past.

"Daddy," she said. "I brought you some supper."

She heard nothing, which meant nothing. He often napped in the spare room, her mother's old sewing room. He hadn't slept in his own bed since his wife died. Janice set the food on the counter and shook her head at the dirty dishes in the sink. She'd be the one to wash them. She called to him again, softer, in case he was sleeping, but the spare room was empty except for the narrow single bed and stacks of her mother's fabric. Bolt ends she'd gotten on sale were leaning in a corner. Janice opened the curtains and lifted the window to relieve the room of stale air. Through the screen she saw her father lying on the ground.

She rushed through the house to the backyard, thinking that he'd had a stroke or a heart attack. She could feel her own heart pounding in her chest. He lay on his back as if taking a rest, a heavy crescent wrench near the curled fingers of his grease-blackened hand. The front of his shirt was matted with dried blood from a gunshot wound. She called the police and began

11

washing the dishes. Nine-one-one was on its way, cops and EMTs and fire trucks. She felt bad for the previous way she'd thought about her father. It was too late now, she knew, but the guilt would live inside her for a long while, like a loose belt on one of the cars in his yard.

CHAPTER TWO

Mick Hardin took his standard two-minute shower, toweled off in one minute, and spent two more getting dressed. His T-shirt was damp against the wet splotches on his torso but he didn't care. He ran his hand over his head to comb his hair, which was already getting longer. He didn't care about that, either. As of 2400 hours last night, he'd ended his status as a serving member of the United States military. He was no longer duty bound to care about anything.

He studied his freshly shaven reflection in the misty mirror. He was thirty-nine years old, still fit, with all his teeth and hair. Not much to brag on, but it was more than a lot of people. If he didn't get too spendy, he could live on his pension for decades. Prior to resignation, he'd agreed to train new CID investigators in exchange for promotion and a commensurate raise. He'd done that for a year. Mick had been surprised to enjoy working with young soldiers but not enough to extend enlistment. He wasn't a teacher, he was an investigator, and now he was unemployed.

Every action seemed significant on his final day in the army — the last shower, the last bed made, the last breakfast of runny eggs, hard toast, and dry potatoes. His final walk from the mess hall to the barracks. His last withdrawal from the bank on base — twenty thousand dollars in cash. Activity on Fort Leonard Wood continued as if nothing important was occurring. To all the other soldiers, nothing was, just another dull day in the service.

He carried a suitcase and a duffel bag to his truck. A corporal gave Mick his final salute, sloppy and quick, the perfunctory gesture indicating a hangover. At the main gate he nodded to the guards and drove north past the ubiquitous enterprises near all garrisons — pawn shop, pizza place, tattoo shop, strip club, and gaming center. Fast food and cheap motels. Fort Leonard Wood was in the Missouri Ozarks, pretty country that reminded Mick of home. He drove northeast to Saint Louis, where he got on I-64 for the long drive east to Rocksalt, Kentucky. The old truck ran well, a 1963 stepside that had belonged to his grandfather, the man who'd raised Mick deep in the Daniel Boone National Forest.

Like all soldiers, he'd dreamed of this day since boot camp. Now it was anticlimactic and depressing. He was grateful to be spared a formal and tedious ceremony requiring stoic endurance. His career had ended with his signature on multiple forms. It was similar to divorce. In both cases, a significant portion of his life stopped abruptly with legal documents in a bland office. He underwent a quick sensation of doubt that he swept aside.

After serving four tours as a combat paratrooper he'd transferred to CID and spent twelve more years tracking down soldiers who'd committed violent felonies. Now he was free, truly free. Free from orders, war, and pressure. Free from emotional responses of victims and their families. Free from making an error with colossal repercussions — the wrong person arrested and a killer still at large.

Mick had a plan for his future, at least the first six months, but he was flexible, ready to shift with any circumstance. No plan survived first contact with the enemy, even if the enemy was civilian life. Affairs had not unfolded the way he'd previously imagined at his retirement — opening a boat rental business on Cave Run Lake and running it with his wife. Now Peggy was living with her new husband and their child. His mother and father were long dead, and the house he'd grown up in had burned to the ground. Mick was going home to a place that was no longer home.

He stopped for gas three times and made it to Rocksalt in ten hours, his speed hampered by the old truck. He'd been gone two years and the town appeared the same — few cars, no pedestrians, the traffic lights blinking both ways at the four intersections. He drove straight to his sister's house. Calling ahead was not a habit with him, a problem at times for his CO, his ex-wife, and his sister. He'd grown up with no telephone and never embraced the widespread use of cell phones. His own was in the glove compartment, turned off. Arriving unannounced had its benefits, especially when taking into custody a young man trained to kill. He no longer needed to think that way but it was deeply ingrained, the same as vigilance toward suspicious objects by the road, a vehicle that followed for too long, or the quick motion of a furtive figure in the shade. The intensity of the habit had kept him alive in war zones. But he understood that it had severely undermined his

16

marriage and he wondered if he was capable of maintaining a close relationship. Neither he nor his sister had ever been very good at it.

Linda lived in their mother's house at the end of Lyons Avenue. It was tidier than his last visit two years ago, freshly painted with new gutters and downspouts. The setting sun glinted off the roof in a steady sheen that suggested new shingles. Maybe she'd gotten a bump in pay after winning the election to sheriff. He went to the side door, but his key wouldn't open the lock. He walked to the front, used only by preachers, politicians, and kids on Halloween. That key didn't work either. He double-checked both doors, then used a penlight to study the locks. They were shiny and new.

He drove to the sheriff's office and parked beside his sister's county-issued SUV. Hand on his door handle, he hesitated. He'd been locked into mission mode so severely that he'd overlooked a detail with negative potential. Two years ago he'd spent his last night in Eldridge County with Sandra Caldwell, who worked as a dispatcher for the sheriff's department. He wondered if she'd been miffed by his sudden departure and subsequent lack of contact. The prospect of seeing her scared him more than facing a barred entry to a village in Afghanistan, knowing it was booby-trapped.

Mick considered calling the office to see if she answered, or calling his sister directly and asking Linda to come outside. Both smacked of cowardice, which he couldn't tolerate. Sandra was probably married by now, or with any luck had quit her job. He left the truck and went to the sheriff's office door, which was locked. He felt a quick sense of gratitude that the staff was gone. He banged on the glass until his sister emerged from her office and let him in.

"Lord love a duck," Linda said, "look what the dogs drug in."

"Hidy, Sis."

"I saw you sitting out there. Getting up the nerve to come in, I bet."

"Something like that."

"Afraid of facing the music on how you treated Sandra?"

"What do you know about that?"

"You leave your truck in front of her house overnight and the whole town knows. Two years is nothing in Eldridge County. Same as two minutes anywhere else."

"Is she mad?"

Linda laughed, a rarity in general, and led him into her office. It was as Spartan as ever — state and national flag, photograph of the governor, desk, filing cabinet, and guest chair. The wall held new adornments — an honorary commission as Kentucky Colonel, an award from the state for meritorious accomplishment, and a special commendation from the FBI.

"Two years," she said. "You look pretty much the same."

"You lost weight."

"A little," she said. "Bought a couple of new uniforms that're supposed to streamline my verticals, whatever that means."

"Well, it works."

"Yeah, until I put on the vest."

They sat looking at each other, not so much an evaluation as a willingness to accept. Each was the only family the other had. Despite their differences — many and extreme — they were loyal in the way of the hills.

"I went by your house," he said. "Keys didn't work."

"I changed the locks."

"Mommy's old ones finally give out?"

"No, they worked."

"Somebody start bothering you over the job?"

"Not your business," she said. "Nothing to do with the job."

"Wrong choice of man?"

19

"Again," she said. "As usual."

Linda shifted in her chair and stared out the window at a small maple. Nothing was happening out there. The humidity draped the leaves with weight that made them droop. Mick knew the topic was over.

"Thanks for taking care of my truck," he said.

"I thought I'd see you when you picked it up."

"I couldn't get away from work. That's why I hired Albin to haul it to base for me. Cost a pretty penny."

"Albin's mixed up in a murder case."

"Albin? That boy wouldn't hit a lick at a snake."

"He's not a suspect. Got a hell of an alibi, too. He was racing at the dirt track in Bluestone. Couple of hundred witnesses."

"How'd he do?" Mick said.

"Took second. Johnny Boy said he'd have won if Pete Lowe was in the pit."

"Don't know him."

"You won't get a chance to. He's the victim. Somebody shot him down in his yard. Daughter found him."

"Well," Mick said. "I'm off the clock now. But if it was me, I'd look at family and friends. Then any woman he was involved with."

"Yep, then neighbors."

Mick nodded.

"You're getting good at sheriffing," he said. "A regular Nancy Drew."

"When are you due back?"

"I'm not. I'm out."

"I don't believe it."

"Yep. Terminated. Retired. Separated from service. It's a complicated process with all kinds of steps. Right now I'm in a period the army calls 'transition to civilian life.' Supposed to be difficult."

Linda leaned back in her chair, swiveled it one way, braced her feet against the floor, then spun all the way around. She had a big smile at the end of the chair's rotation, as if the spin had obliterated the years. Mick hadn't seen the joyous side of her in a long time. It was worth the trip.

"Damn!" she said. "Twenty years went fast. You here for good?"

"I'd like to stay with you for a few days, if you ain't caring."

"Okay."

"Then I'm moving to France. Got a six-month lease."

"What? Why France?"

"I speak enough of it to get by. Can't talk to a banker or understand a word on the phone, but I can order food and go to stores."

"Do they talk English?"

"They say they don't, but a lot do. When they hear how bad my accent is, most folks switch to English."

"Do they sound like Pepé Le Pew?"

"Oh, yeah," he said. "The whole country is filled with cartoon skunks. You know what I never understood? Why a French skunk had a Spanish first name."

"Reckon you'll have plenty of time to figure that out."

Mick nodded. He'd missed talking to his sister, to someone who knew him well. The only others were dead or no longer in his life. There was plenty of precedent in the hills for brother and sister to live together in the family home, but it wouldn't suit him — or her. Both were too fixed in their ways. On the other hand, his presence might prevent her from changing the locks to keep a man out of her house. But it was none of his business.

"Seriously," she said, "why are you here?"

"To say goodbye to you, Sis."

"Nothing else?"

"I'll put my truck in storage somewhere so it doesn't sit in front of your house. It might not go with your new locks."

Linda snatched a sheet of paper from her desk, crumpled it quickly into a ball, and threw it at him. Mick shifted his head and it flew over his shoulder.

"Used to," he said, "you'd have thrown a paperweight."

"Yeah, well, time affects everybody different. We're getting mature."

"I've never known you to be philosophical."

"It's the job," she said. "I used to think everything was simple, black and white, legal and illegal. Now it's a lot more complicated. What's lawful, what's justice, and what's best for the community. Sometimes they overlap but not often enough."

Mick nodded. Two years was the longest period he'd gone without seeing his sister. He wondered if it had been a crucial time for her. When change happened, it was incremental. Then the results appeared suddenly like the overnight success of a musician who'd been playing gigs for fifteen years.

Mick gestured to the framed certificates on the wall.

"What's all that?" he said.

"The usual bullshit."

"Then why put them up?"

"Politics, Big Bro. Never know who might

walk in here."

"You're learning."

"Yeah, the hard way. Made some enemies, too."

"As long as your friends have more juice than your enemies, you're doing good."

"Sometimes it's hard to know who's who in that book."

"It's more like an Etch A Sketch than a book," Mick said. "Remember those? Turn it upside down and shake it and the screen goes blank. That's politics."

Linda took a set of keys from her purse, removed one, and slid it across the desk.

"I'll meet you there later. I've got to wait for the night dispatcher and do paperwork. There's half a sub in the fridge."

"Maybe I'll eat with Johnny Boy," he said.

"He's at the Bluestone Speedway talking to people who knew the victim. It's race night and they'll all be there. Easier than traipsing around four counties hunting them down."

He picked up the key.

"Thanks," he said.

"Don't be messing with my stuff."

He nodded, grinned, and left.

CHAPTER THREE

Like most boys in eastern Kentucky, Johnny Boy Tolliver had grown up enamored of racing, steeped in stories of powerful muscle cars. He and his grade school buddies drew pictures of the race cars they'd own, choosing personal color schemes. Learning to drive at age fifteen initiated a shift. He was careful behind the wheel, stricken by the responsibility of feet, hands, and eyes working together to operate a dangerous machine. He wrecked three times, minor brushes with two ditches and a tree. Instead of being emboldened by the experience, he became more cautious. He never had another accident.

At age seventeen he went to the Bluestone Speedway because a particular girl was going, too. Stock cars drove a dirt oval, producing a roar on the straightaways and filling the air with dust. The combination of noise and dirt irritated Johnny Boy, compounded by supreme disappointment — the girl he liked was there for a driver whose car left the race with a blown engine. She went straight to the pit and Johnny Boy went straight home.

He hadn't been back to Bluestone until now, and not much had changed. People still ate hot dogs, drank Cokes infused with bourbon, and smoked left-handed cigarettes in the parking lot. Scruffy young men stared at sexy women who clung to the arms of tough older men. The noise and dust pervaded everything. He was ready to leave and he'd only talked to a few people who knew the dead man.

Pete Lowe was considered the finest mechanic at the track, hard to get along with in general, and worse after his wife died. He'd worked at numerous garages in three counties — Eldridge, Fleming, and Bath — but always got mad over something trivial and quit. No one had ever fired Pete Lowe. His abilities with an engine bordered on the mysterious, as if he was attuned to a layer of ethereal understanding that eluded everyone else. He could diagnose a problem after five seconds of listening to a motor. One sniff of a carburetor and he knew the precise adjustment necessary for the fuel injection. He kept a thumbnail filed at an angle and used it to perfectly calibrate spark plug points. When it came to engines, he was keen as a briar. Everyone wanted him in their pit.

Johnny Boy was tired of hearing about him. The old adage "don't speak ill of the dead" carried a lot of weight in the hills. You could be in the middle of cussing a man up one side and down the other but if he keeled over dead, you immediately shifted to voluminous praise, as if an apostle had died. The worst thing Johnny Boy heard about Pete came from a large man with a deep voice who said, "Pete's Pete." Johnny Boy was wasting his time and getting low-spirited. He recalled his rejection as a teenager. That woman now had four kids and a third husband. If she'd married Johnny Boy, they'd still be together and he'd be happy. He was disgusted with everything — the absurd attention on automobiles going in circles and getting nowhere, the dust and noise and drunken fans, his own past, and most of all himself. He left and headed for Rocksalt, driving five miles under the speed limit.

The interstate was much faster but he took Old 60 in honor of a classmate who drove three races. Chad had loved Mustangs as a kid and driven them despite their lack of acceleration at crucial times. He'd painted his race car the same as he'd drawn it in the fourth grade, with the number 8 in a blue circle. Johnny Boy remembered him saying that eight was his favorite number because if you turned it sideways it was the sign for infinity, and eventually every race car wound up sideways. Chad never took the interstate because, as he said, he was an oval man, not a drag racer. He preferred driving on Highway 60 for the curves. One night someone called about a wreck and the police found the car easily. They searched all night for Chad, then visited nearby houses, figuring that he'd gotten hurt and was wandering around. The morning mist lifted and the police saw his body in a tree, flung from the car.

Johnny Boy knew he was too young to dwell on the past. People in the hills often died early. By age thirty everyone knew several people in the cemetery. It occurred to him that was the reason hill people revered the dead. There were too many for such a small population.

At a crossroad he stopped for gas at the twenty-four-hour place that had put a family-owned station out of business. He shook his head at such thinking — more of the past. It didn't make sense to lament the loss of a gas station while sticking the nozzle of a pump into his fuel tank. To cheer himself he went inside for a bottle of Dr Pepper. Behind the counter was a short woman, lithe and quick moving. Every visible part of her body was tattooed except her face, and Johnny Boy supposed that the smaller you were, the cheaper it was to cover all your skin. A big man would need a second job to cover his tattoo bills.

Outside he completed the automated transaction for gas while watching an old Jeep Wagoneer drive to the farthest pump. A man got out, looked around as if hunting a lost cat, and stepped into the glare of LED light above the pumps. He had a beard and long hair, an unusual combination for the hills, out of fashion. Young boys were bringing back the long beard but kept their hair short, copying styles off television. The man didn't look old enough to be a former hippie stuck in his own past.

Johnny Boy started his car and drove past the man, giving him a quick glance, then slowing for a long stare. The man looked up and Johnny Boy studied him. Something about him was familiar. It wasn't from a previous arrest or a face on a state BOLO alert. It could be nothing more than a family resemblance to people Johnny Boy saw every day. Still, it scratched around in the back of his mind like a rat in a corn crib. It was the eyes, he thought. It had to be the eyes since little else was visible. Not the color but the bone structure, the brow and cheekbones. He knew those features. He wished he'd taken down the license plate number of the man's car.

Rocksalt was a college town, which meant hundreds of shoddy rentals, small houses for junior professors, and a few streets with fancy homes for doctors, lawyers, and university administrators. Johnny Boy lived in a four-room apartment in one of the few buildings intended for working adults. He'd been saving for a house, but didn't know where he wanted to live. He figured his eventual wife would influence the decision, but he hadn't married, didn't have a girl-friend, and his last date was three years ago.

He sat in his favorite chair — the only chair — and wondered if he was depressed. He concluded that wondering about it indicated that he wasn't. Truly depressed people just sat or slept or drifted in a mental fog. During the last twenty years, the aver-age life span of people in the hills had decreased and he wondered if that pulled back a midlife crisis. He was twenty-six. Maybe this was the onset — negative self-evaluation, boredom with his meaningless life, and chronic reminiscence. He was weary of his own safe routines. Something needed to change, but he had no idea what. He liked his job and didn't want to live anywhere else. What did that leave?

CHAPTER FOUR

Still on army time, Mick awoke just before dawn and decided to make breakfast for his sister before she went to work. He lay in bed looking around the room he'd slept in until age eight, when he'd gone to live with his grandfather in the woods. His mother had devoted herself to her daughter but Linda had moved out at age eighteen for a tiny apartment, a job, and classes at Rocksalt College. Their mother turned increasingly inward, rarely leaving the house, concerned exclusively with time and weather. Her house contained more than sixty clocks and dozens of calendars. Visible through each window was a thermometer. Her large TV was tuned perpetually to a twenty-four-hour weather channel. She died watching a mudslide in Burma. Linda inherited the house.

He made coffee and began preparing the single meal he knew how to make, taught to him by his grandfather — eggs, bacon, potatoes, and toast. Over the years he'd added omelets and poached eggs to his repertoire but today he stuck with the classic formula of fry, flip, and slide.

He heard the bathroom door close and added diced onions to the potatoes. A few minutes later, Linda entered the kitchen with an amiable grunt and poured a cup of coffee. Mick always woke up like a hound dog ready to run but Linda operated on a slower schedule. He made her a plate and they ate silently. After a second cup of coffee she was awake enough to talk.

"Are you really out?" she said. "For good?"

"Yeah."

"Why?"

"Got my twenty in. I can live on the pension. Every year there's thousands of new recruits. They're the same age but I get older."

"I'd say you got time figured out pretty good," she said. "It's a special day, you should mark it on the calendar if you can find one around here."

She smiled, the first of the day, and Mick figured probably the last. He nodded.

"Have you talked to Peggy?" he said.

"Don't put me in the middle. Mom tried

33

that with me and Dad, then me and you. I didn't then and I won't now. If you want to talk, give her a call."

"Is she still with that guy?"

"Yeah, they had another kid. And I'm done on the subject."

Linda finished her coffee and went to her room. Mick cleaned the kitchen. She returned wearing her uniform and duty belt, hair pulled back and folded into a neat bun. She had car keys in one hand and a ballistic vest in the other.

"You always wear one?" Mick said.

"On a call, yeah. Supposed to stop any handgun. What'd you wear?"

"Level four with ceramic plates. Good against rifles and shrapnel. That's one thing I won't miss. Way too hot in the desert for that gear."

"They work though, right?"

"Fewer casualties. But more soldiers lose limbs and get head wounds."

"What's your agenda for the day?" she said. "Drive around and get sad?"

Mick nodded. She stared at him and he understood that she was waiting for him to offer more information. It was an old trick, one he'd utilized hundreds of times. It meant she was learning on the job or had received training. He could outwait her,

34

initiate a new subject, or simply leave the room. He was trying to figure out which would piss her off the least, when she spoke.

"Thanks for breakfast," she said and left.

Mick drove east of town, stopping for gas at Haney's Tire and Bible, a station run for thirty years by a family of redheads that went gray early. He'd known three generations worth, all named some version of Joe. A dark-haired man in his early twenties sauntered out to the truck, a feed-store hat cocked at an angle and a tire gauge clipped to his shirt.

"New owners?" Mick said.

"Naw. Everybody thinks that on account of my black hair. I'm Joey. Your tires look new. Must be wanting gas or a Bible."

"Fill it up."

Mick cut the engine and watched Joey, unable to recall the last time a gas station attendant had topped off his tank. It was a dying occupation, same as typewriter repairmen and shorthand secretaries. In forty years, Joey would be sitting around telling stories of the old days before electric cars put Haney's out of business.

Mick paid cash and drove away, thinking about the circumstance of having dark hair in a family of gingers. Either somebody married out or a black-headed gene had finally worked its way to the fore. He pondered his lack of knowledge about genetics in general, then shook his head to clear his mind. Leaving the army had eliminated the need for a rigidity of thought, but he didn't like how all manner of idea poured into the gap. His thinking was screwy. The day's mission was to visit the only property he owned, left to him by his grandfather. He figured he was saying goodbye, although he was unsure to what. His grandfather, his past, or the land he loved? Maybe to himself.

The dirt lane ran up the hill and out a ridge so overgrown that he parked and walked. It was less a road than a mile-long driveway of dirt and brush that had regrown since Mick cleared it two years ago. Every sweetgum stump had sprouted a dozen saplings, as if angry at having been cut down and determined to marshal reinforcements. It was the only tree his grandfather had disliked.

At the top of the hill, Mick rested momentarily, admiring the small plateau at the end of a narrow ridge surrounded by thick woods. A pair of blue jays hollered a warning that an intruder had appeared. Smaller birds rose from the trees and fled. Mick approached the remnants of the cabin he'd grown up in. A fire had gutted it two years back, leaving blackened holes for doors and windows, a stone chimney, and little else. The roof and porch had burned. Only the four walls remained, constructed of heavy timbers notched at the ends to interlock. They'd withstood a hundred years of weather and now fire. He used a stick to pick through the debris, vaguely searching for any scrap of his past — a lucky rock, a railroad spike, a coffee pot. He found nothing. The thick layer of ash was matted from rain. A poplar grew in the living room.

He returned to his truck and drove to town. A new Dollar General and a chain gas station had appeared where the old drive-in movie theater had been. He pulled over, called his sister's cell phone, and asked if she was at the sheriff's station.

"Sure not," Linda said. "I'm out in the county talking to Pete Lowe's neighbors. Not too many and spread out."

"How about Johnny Boy? He there?"

"No, he's still tracking down the race crew Pete worked for. He did talk to Albin, who asked about you. Said he heard you were in."

"How's that possible? It's been less than twelve hours."

"You forgot how Rocksalt is," she said. "You can sneeze in town and the spray will beat you back to the house."

"You got that off Papaw."

"And a few other good ones."

"I was just up at the cabin," he said. "What's left of it."

"Guaranteed to make you sad. Maybe you should join the army or something. Get some purpose in your life."

Mick nodded.

"You're nodding, aren't you?" she said. "Why do you want to know where Johnny Boy and me are at? Let me guess. Your next plan is to visit Sandra and you want to make sure she's alone in the office."

Mick nodded.

"Nod all you want," she said. "That's about like going to the cabin, only you'll be sad and have to talk to her. See you later."

She ended the call and Mick stared at his phone. Linda was right on all counts. The futility of his plan would increase a growing sense of melancholy. He drove to the sheriff's office, gathered his courage, and got out of the truck. Sandra left the station and locked the door behind her. Momentarily discombobulated, he forced himself forward as if to morning muster roll call after a night of drinking. Her expression was blank.

"Hey, Sandra."

"Hidy, Mick."

He glanced at the eastern hills. The dark treeline was a rickrack trim against the pale sky. Across the lot came the guttural sound of men talking, then a laugh that trailed away.

"I should have written a note," he said.

"A note?"

"Yeah. When I, uh, left your house."

"Two years ago?"

Mick nodded.

"You're worried about a note?" she said.

"Yes. It would be right. Would've been, I mean."

"You disappeared. Linda didn't know where you were. Nobody did."

"My flight was out of Detroit. I had to drive up there, get a room, and leave the next day."

"A phone call or a text would have been good."

"You're right. I didn't think of that. Detroit was complicated. Then I was back on base in Germany. Figured you'd not want to hear from me."

"You figured wrong," she said.

"I usually do with women. I told you that."

"What you told me was that your grandfather didn't teach you anything about women except to be nice, listen, and carry heavy things."

Mick nodded, surprised at her memory. It was from a brief conversation in his truck on their first date. That had been a mistake, as was coming here now. Everything he'd ever done as a civilian had been a mistake. He only excelled in the service, following orders, tasked with a specific mission.

"Well," he said. "I'm sorry."

He turned to leave. He had his hand on the truck's door handle when she spoke.

"Mick," she said. "You hungry? I'm on my way to lunch."

"Little early for me."

"Never too early for tacos. I'll drive. It's a new place. You'll like it."

"Can you leave?"

"Yeah, I've got two cell phones now. All calls to the station get forwarded. The other phone is mine with the number you apparently lost."

He climbed in the passenger seat of her car, further bamboozled by their interaction. He wasn't hungry but he'd never been able to say no to any woman, another lesson from his grandfather. His ex-wife had figured it out but rarely asked for anything. Then she asked for a divorce.

"How's your uncle?" he said.

"He passed."

"Sorry to hear that. Recently?"

She gave him a hard glance.

"In the past two years," she said.

Preferring to avoid another faux pas, he remained silent as they drove through town. A few people sat at tables outside the old movie theater that had been converted to a coffee shop and bookstore. Two doors down was a bar situated where a junk store had been run by a man who was legendary for locking customers inside until they bought something. He died the richest man in town. His grave had a mailbox on a post to receive overdue payments.

Sandra drove to an empty lot with a brightly painted vehicle, half truck and half van, that said: ROCKIN' TACOS. Next to it were four picnic tables. Sandra parked and Mick followed her to the food truck. A wide window had a hatch propped open to shade a ledge that held napkins and condiments.

"Hey, Ray-Ray," she said. "Y'all open yet?"

A head shaped like the end of a howitzer shell appeared in the serving window. Raymond Kissick gave Sandra a broad smile then settled his expression as he took in Mick. The two men regarded each other without speaking. Raymond was a marine who'd recently returned to Eldridge County. The last time Mick saw him was after an illegal mission of vengeance for Raymond's brothers. Mick had never spoken of it to anyone and figured Raymond hadn't, either.

A voice accented by the US southern border shouted from the truck.

"We're not ready yet, Reymundo!"

"It's Sandy," Raymond said.

A succession of noises issued from the vehicle, pans and cutlery clanging, then a door slammed and a man rushed around the truck. Small and agile, he had shiny black hair cut short and modified on the sides by a razor. He hugged Sandra, kissed her on the cheek, and faced Mick.

"And who's this, Sandra?" he said. "*¿Un amante?* Your new boyfriend?"

"No," Sandra said. "No way."

"*Hola,*" Mick said. "*¿Cómo estás?*"

"*Estoy bien, gracias por preguntar. ¿Tienes hambre? Cualquier cosa por Sandra.*"

"*Casa. Cuchillo. Gato. Indoro.* That's all the Spanish I know. And some cuss words. I'm Mick."

He offered his hand and they shook gravely.

"I am Juan Carlos. You are a friend of Raymond. He told me of you. *El soldado.*"

"Not anymore," Mick said. "I retired."

"Ah, you have no home."

Raymond had left the truck and was walk-

42

ing across the gravel.

"How's your mom?" Mick said.

"Better," Raymond said. "It's still hard but she loves J.C."

"Yes," Juan Carlos said. "Mama Shifty loves me more than you."

He returned to the truck. Mick watched an old car trundle by, its bumper wired in place at an angle. Raymond and Sandra had gone to high school together, continuing their friendship when he returned after twenty-five years in the Corps.

"You really out?" Raymond said.

Mick nodded.

"Miss it yet?"

"No, but this morning I thought about re-enlisting."

"Boot camp at forty," Raymond said. He laughed, a shrill sound in the still air.

They sat at a picnic table, Mick and Raymond instinctively facing the road. Three sparrows studied them from a maple. At the far edge of the lot, a brown-and-yellow cat watched the birds. A truck drove by and honked. Raymond waved a greeting.

"You're fitting in pretty good," Mick said.

"That boy used to beat on me in high school. Now he's scared to."

"How's Juan Carlos doing around here?"

"They like his food but don't know what

43

to make of him."

"Because he's gay or Mexican? Or both?"

"Mainly because he's Catholic."

"I like him," Sandra said. "He's got everyone in Rocksalt eating out of his hand. Literally."

Juan Carlos deftly carried paper plates with tacos, beans, rice, and guacamole to the table. They ate silently. As the sun rose above the hill, the shadow retreated east like a line of surf when the tide went out. Mick finished one taco and started on the second.

"Would you like two more?" Juan Carlos said.

"Yes and no," Mick said. "I could eat six more but I'll hold off. It's the cheese that makes it great."

Juan Carlos made an expression of approval.

"Yes," he said. "It is queso Oaxaca. Traditional."

"Where do you get it?" Sandra said. "I never saw it at the IGA."

"Mexington," Juan Carlos said.

"It's a neighborhood in Lexington," Raymond said. "We drive up there once a week and stock up. Only place to get corn tortillas. J.C. knows the best places to shop."

"There is a bar we like," Juan Carlos said. "If we drink too much we stay in a hotel.

We have a wonderful time. You two should join us."

"No," Sandra said. Her voice was firm with no trace of politesse.

Juan Carlos lifted his eyebrows and smiled.

"It is like a telenovela," he said. "You two will make up after the third commercial. It is always a long one, the third. You are supposed to hope for the people while the TV tries to sell you something."

Mick stared at his plate. He wondered if they'd reached the first commercial yet, if he could leave the country before the third one. He shook his head quickly to clear his mind. He'd stepped into Juan Carlos's metaphor, accepted it as real, and engaged in its aftermath. In less than twenty-four hours of civilian life, he was already over his head.

Two cars drove into the lot. Juan Carlos sprang from the table, circled the food truck, and appeared in the open window.

"Nobody gives him any trouble?" Mick said.

"Not with me around," Raymond said. "How long you in for?"

"Couple of days."

"Heard you were moving to Europe," Sandra said.

Mick nodded.

"Where?" Raymond said.

"Corsica."

Another vehicle entered the makeshift lot, then a fourth. Raymond stood and gathered the paper plates, plastic forks, and napkins.

"Got to earn my keep," he said.

"Thought it was the other way around," Mick said.

"Not according to Mommy and J.C."

He left, giving a standard wave to a car, a quick sideways motion, arm low, hand slightly uplifted. Mick hadn't seen it in so long he'd forgotten it. It had been his grand-father's lifelong greeting, a gesture of acknowledgment without beckoning com-pany.

"Corsica," Sandra said. "You got a girl-friend living there?"

"I know one guy. Sebastien. A British soldier who retired there."

"Then why go?"

"It reminds me of here. Beautiful country, good people, old-fashioned way of living. If you're in a foreign country, being an out-sider is normal. I never fit in here, Sandra. In Corsica, it doesn't matter."

The line at the window was seven people long. A van parked and the driver disem-barked. Raymond carried out a cardboard box, collected payment, and returned to the taco truck. Three more vehicles arrived and the line deepened.

"They're getting busy," Sandra said. "We should give this table up."

Mick stood and they walked to her car.

"Ray-Ray's doing all right," she said. "He cheered up when Juan Carlos moved here."

"How could you tell?"

"I've known him a long time," she said. "Talk about not fitting in. Try being him, from his family. Gay people have it hard here."

"They have it hard everywhere."

They looked at each other briefly in mutual agreement. More birds had gathered in the trees, waiting for scraps. An intrepid crow was cautiously pecking at the ground like a recon for his flock. Someone laughed and the crow flew to a sycamore.

"I got to get back to work," Sandra said. "You coming?"

"Naw, I'll help Raymond."

Sandra opened her car door, got in, and started the engine. Mick went to the food truck and washed dishes in a cramped space until the lunch rush dwindled. Twice Juan Carlos returned pans with an infinitesimal speck of hardened gristle Mick had missed. He finished, went outside, removed his

47

shirt, and draped it over a picnic table. Raymond joined him.

"Stripping down," he said. "Didn't take you long to get back into the local way of life. Half the boys around here carry a shirt in their car so they can go in a gas station for smokes."

"Give me a ride? My truck's at the station."

"Can't do it. We stay here till four, then set up in town. Catch people getting off work and college students. I'll call you a cab."

Raymond went to the food truck. Mick watched the crow chase three robins away from a tattered fragment of tortilla. The crow finished the tortilla then marched in a circle as if guarding the area. A robin waited on the periphery. Mick understood the motivation of both birds. They could fly anywhere but, like Mick, they'd always return to a familiar sight.

A taxi entered the lot and stopped beside him.

"Mick," said the driver. "Is that you? Hey, man. Are you my fare? That's great. I'll take you anywhere. I heard you were in."

Mick got in the car.

"Hidy, Albin," he said. "This a new rig?"

"Yeah. They hired more people and I got

upped. You're looking at the top driver in a fleet of three."

"Take me to the station."

Mick braced himself for Albin's standard speed, but he drove the three miles like a man who'd lost his glasses. Walking would've been faster.

"Being mighty careful," Mick said.

"Got to be. Can't risk nothing now that I'm driving at Bluestone. I told you I was going to one day."

"What I remember was you thinking I was a race promoter."

"Yeah, well, turns out I didn't need a promoter, I needed a car. Three of us put in shares and take turns driving. I took second last week. We put the winnings back into the car but you get to keep your own trophy. I got mine setting on a special shelf. Want to see it? I got a picture on my phone."

"Not while you're driving. My sister might cite you for reckless."

Albin lifted his foot from the accelerator. The car slowed immediately but continued as if the idle was high. A standard shift such as Mick's truck would have stalled.

"I was kidding," Mick said.

"I can't be too careful. Especially after Johnny Boy asked me a thousand questions. You hear about Pete? Johnny Boy thinks I killed him."

"Did you?"

"Hell, no! Pete Lowe was the reason I placed in them races. He tuned that car like a fiddle and it ran like a sewing machine."

"Johnny Boy's a pretty good lawman," Mick said.

"I heard that. But he talks a lot."

"So do you, Albin. Figured you'd like to talk to a man who likes to talk."

They arrived at the sheriff's station and Albin parked beside Mick's truck.

"What do I owe you?" Mick said.

"Do me a favor and nothing."

"I'd rather settle up."

Mick gave him a ten-dollar bill.

"It's my cousin," Albin said. "He's getting evicted. Today's the last day he can stay where he's at. I'm hoping you'll say something to your sister."

"Didn't pay the rent?"

"It ain't like that," Albin said. "A whole lot worser."

"The bank? You can't fight them."

"His dad."

Johnny Boy came out of the building and walked to Albin's car.

"Just the feller I wanted to see," Johnny Boy said. "Who you got with you? Hey,

Mick, I heard you were in. You doing all right?"

Mick nodded.

"Albin," Johnny Boy said, "you got four uncles, right?"

"Five."

"The one I want is Bill-Tom Reeder. Up on Crosscut Ridge."

"No, he moved to Redbird. The one on Crosscut is Uncle Hank."

"Which one's got a boy named Roscoe?"

"That's Bill-Tom."

"Well, he's wanting Roscoe off his property."

"I done heard," Albin said. "I was just telling Mick about it. Maybe he can help."

"Good idea," Johnny Boy said. "Come on, Mick. We'll take my car."

"You don't need me," Mick said.

"I might. Evictions can get tricky."

"What about Linda?"

"She's off interviewing Pete Lowe's neighbors."

Mick felt caught in a crossfire. Both men wanted his help but in a different direction. The smart thing would be to get in his truck and drive. But go where? Back to his sister's and watch television? He left the cab and went to his truck for his cell phone. Behind him he heard Albin and Johnny Boy laugh-

51

ing. Mick called the airline to book an earlier flight to Corsica but there were none available.

CHAPTER FIVE

Mick and Johnny Boy drove through Rocksalt, founded in the widest spot between the hills. A former rail town for extraction industries, it was now home to a hospital and a college at opposite ends of town. Johnny Boy slowed at a gas station to study the customers.

"You looking for somebody?" Mick said.

"Yes and no. I'm looking but I don't know for who. I saw a face a few days ago I thought I recognized. It's been bugging me."

"Two places everybody goes — gas stations and drug stores. If they're traveling, they hit fast food and laundromats."

Johnny Boy made a quick turn and cruised past a low white building with a sign that said:

COIN LAUNDRY
WE TAKE BEAKER BUCKS

53

Three cars sat in the lot. A young woman carried a plastic basket to a car, shifted the weight to her hip, and opened the back door. Johnny Boy squinted out the window then shook his head.

"No good," he said. "They're all Eldridge County plates."

"What are beaker bucks?"

"Some kind of college thing. Pop machines take them."

Mick nodded. West of town they passed a family sawmill that had been converted to a store selling artisanal sausage. An old hound lying in the shade lifted its head to track the passage of the truck, then settled back on its crossed paws.

"Dog was fat for an outside dog," Johnny Boy said.

"Probably from eating sausage. You ever try theirs?"

"I don't eat anything artisanal. Just a way to charge more money. You know they got artisanal potato chips? Supposed to fry one batch at a time. Then what? They throw out the oil? They don't even do that after a cremation. I got a buddy works at one of those places. He said they don't clean the hopper between bodies. You get a baggie full of ash that's your grandma and whoever else got burnt up that week."

"Maybe you should open an artisanal crematorium."

Mick was joking but Johnny Boy mulled it over for several minutes, providing a pleasant break in the conversation.

"Nope," Johnny Boy said. "I'm not fooling with cremation. Could be ghosts. That's why they're gray colored, from the ashes."

They were out of town now, having left the main road for a narrow blacktop lane with a ditch on one side.

"Any luck with Albin's mechanic?" Mick said.

"No. It's an investigative pickle. Pete Lowe didn't have any friends but no enemies, either. Linda's got a couple more days of talking to neighbors."

"Why's it taking so long?"

"Every one of them's on a rough road, up hills and down hollers. To get to one house takes a while. Then all the way back to the Main Road, find the next turnoff, and start again. Sometimes they're not home. If it rains, you got to wait for the creek to go down to cross. It rained last night."

Johnny Boy slowed for a turn onto a dirt road that climbed a hill. They passed two trailers and a semi-collapsed barn. The brick circle of an aboveground well was covered by an old refrigerator with no door. Mick grinned at the practicality, a staple of hill culture.

"Tell me what we're getting into," Mick said.

"Eviction is all I know."

"You got the papers?"

"It's a family thing. No rent, no lease. Linda wants me to find out what's going on and head off any trouble."

Mick nodded, thinking about Albin's request to put in a word. He hoped it wasn't a boy dealing drugs out of his folks' house. The road crested at a large oak and Johnny Boy parked. They walked down the dirt lane past a small, well-built structure with a window covered by chicken wire. It had a green roof of sheet metal and two steps to the entrance.

At the end of the driveway was another house. Shaded by a large maple was a Bronco with the hood up. The front door of the house opened and a man in his early fifties emerged. He wore jeans, boots, and a cotton work shirt with the sleeves rolled up.

"Mr. Reeder?" Johnny Boy said.

"Sure am," the man said. "You law?"

Johnny Boy pointed at his vehicle up the hill.

"Yep. Deputy."

"Can't see that far without my glasses,"

Mr. Reeder said. "I don't need them in the house. They get away from me."

"My aunt keeps hers on a cord around her neck."

"Tried that with a shoestring. Damn things swung into my eggs. I eat eggs every day. Used to anyhow but not no more. That's why I called you."

"Over eggs?" Johnny Boy said.

"About my boy living in the chicken house."

He pointed at the well-built structure. Johnny Boy looked at it for a full minute before speaking.

"That is the nicest chicken house I ever did see," Johnny Boy said.

"That's what Roscoe said. I want him out."

"Is he in there now?"

"Yep, him and his wife both."

"They're living in there?"

"Sure damn are. They turned my chickens loose and every last one of them died."

"Your boy kill them?" Johnny Boy said.

"No, he wouldn't hurt nothing. Too lazy to shoo a bee. Neighbor dogs got some of my hens. Fox and owl at night. I seen a hawk take one right there."

Mr. Reeder pointed at a nondescript area of his yard and bowed his head as if honoring a significant historical site.

"Anybody live with you, Mr. Reeder?"

"No. My wife moved in with a plumber from Carter County four years ago. Had me a girlfriend last month but I don't know, I just don't know."

"What don't you know?"

"Where she's at."

Mick watched an indigo bunting cut a blue line through the air to a low limb and emit its cheerful call. This was a side to Johnny Boy he'd never seen, the reason he was a good deputy. Linda would have been frustrated by now. Johnny Boy was just getting warmed up.

"Well," Johnny Boy said, "it seems like you got an easy fix. Tell your boy to move in with you."

"I done did. He flat won't."

"Is there something he's up to that he don't want you knowing about?"

"Like what? He don't do a damn thing."

"Ain't saying your boy is one," Johnny Boy said. "But they's some people to cook meth and sell it."

"I wish he would. Right now he ain't worth two crawdads. My brother told me I should've raised him like a dog, then sell him and get ahead."

"Is he all right? I mean, has he been feeling low or anything?"

"My brother? He takes heart pills."

"I meant your son."

"Naw, Roscoe's right sprightly when he comes over for food."

"Say he's eating with you?"

"Not exactly. I make a couple of plates for him and he takes them. His wife is finicky. Sardines and tuna's about all she likes."

"Uh-huh," Johnny Boy said. "I got to ask you a couple of official questions. Don't take them the wrong way. Situation like this, it's got to be legal. That all right with you?"

"I ain't a'caring."

"Do you have any reason to be afraid of your son?"

"Afraid of Roscoe? Hell, no."

"Did he threaten you? Abuse you in any way?"

"No, sir."

"Do you own this property?"

"Yep."

"Is any of it in your son's name? Or anyone else's?"

"No, it's mine. All of it. You can shoot a bullet any direction and it'll land on Reeder dirt."

The slight wind shifted and a breeze carried the ammonia smell of chicken manure across the yard. Johnny Boy removed a handkerchief from his pocket. He wiped his eyes and blew his nose, then carefully folded the cloth and tucked it away.

"Mr. Reeder," Mick said. "Does your son have a gun in there?"

"He pawned his rifle but might have a pistol. There's two baby roosters in there, too."

"If they're babies," Mick said, "how do you know they're roosters?"

"They ain't chicks, they're just little."

"Do I have your permission to enter the chicken house?" Johnny Boy said.

"Yes, damn it, that's why I called you."

Johnny Boy crossed the thick grass and knocked on the door.

"Roscoe," he said. "You in there? It's Deputy Tolliver."

From inside came a man's voice, slightly muffled by the wood walls.

"That you, Johnny Boy?"

"Yeah."

"I ain't talking to no lawman. Who's that other feller?"

"Just a buddy."

Johnny Boy looked at Mick and pointed to the door.

"I'm Jimmy Hardin's boy, Mick. Can I come in?"

"Door's open. Ain't no lock to it."

60

"You got ary a gun I ort to know about?"

"Yeah, somewhere."

Mick stepped past Johnny Boy, pushed the door open, and entered. The smell was much stronger. He breathed through his mouth, letting his vision adjust to the dark room. He opened the door wider to allow light inside. The dim figure of a man stood in the back.

"Shut the damn door," Roscoe said.

"Too dark. You got a light?"

Roscoe moved and a floor lamp illuminated the space. Mick closed the door. The single room contained a microwave, a couch with bedding, a chair, and a laptop computer. Built into three walls were empty nesting boxes separated by panels. Standing in the corner was a younger replica of Mr. Reeder — same clothes, haircut, and build. He cradled a small rooster gently against his chest. Mick figured that Roscoe posed no threat unless he threw the bird at him.

"Your wife here?" Mick said.

"She's been gone awhile. I told Daddy she was still here so he'd leave me alone. He respects a lady's privacy."

"Mind if I sit down?"

"If you want to. Might be chicken dooky on it."

Mick moved to the chair and sat, stretching his legs out casually.

"Clothes'll wash," he said. "I sat in worse."

"You lived in a chicken house, too?"

"No. I was in the army."

"I thought about the army," Roscoe said. "But I didn't want to leave out of here."

"Well, they got barracks better than this."

"I mean the hills, not the chicken house."

"I understand," Mick said. "I couldn't wait to leave here. Then couldn't wait to get back. Now I don't know what I want."

"What are you doing with Johnny Boy anyhow? I never knowed him to have many friends."

"I don't, either," Mick said. "Guess me and him got to take who we can."

Roscoe shuffled across the floor and eased the rooster into a wire cage. He spoke softly in a high voice as if talking to an infant.

"Here ya go, Tiger," he said. "You're all right. I'll be right here talking for a minute. Go on and get you something to drink."

The rooster lifted its head, looked about as if seeking escape, then strutted three steps to a water bowl. Roscoe closed the cage door and latched it.

"Is that thing full-grown?" Mick said.

"Yeah, that breed runs to the little."

A rustling sound came from a dusky corner. Mick saw a flicker of movement in the shadows.

"You got another one?" Mick said.

"Maybe. Why?"

"No reason."

"Just so you know," Roscoe said, "I ain't leaving out of here and Tiger ain't for sale."

"What about the other one?"

"Charles ain't mine. You can tell Johnny Boy I didn't steal him, either."

"Who's Charles belong to?"

"Pete Lowe."

"Pete the mechanic?"

"Yeah, he brought it over here. Asked me to keep it for him."

"When was this?"

"Three days ago. Maybe a week. I don't know. I'm running on chicken time."

"I need to go out for a minute," Mick said.

"Make sure that door shuts tight."

Mick nodded. He went outside and gestured for Johnny Boy. They walked far enough away from Mr. Reeder to talk privately. Mick told him about Charles.

"Pete Lowe's bird?" Johnny Boy said. "Maybe Roscoe killed him and stole Charles. But then why would Roscoe tell you whose bird it was? No, that's not the case. We need to talk to Mr. Reeder."

"Good idea."

Mr. Reeder was bent over an oily wooden

63

toolbox beside the Bronco. He held a socket wrench four inches from his face. He showed it to Johnny Boy.

"Is that a seven-eighths?" he said. "I can't hardly make it out."

"Sure is," Johnny Boy said. "Did Pete Lowe come by here?"

"Yeah."

"Did he have anything with him?"

"A cardboard box. Gave it to Roscoe."

"When was this exactly?"

"Last Wednesday evening."

"You sure about that?"

"Yeah, the church bells were ringing down the holler for services," Mr. Reeder said. "Reach me a piece of wire."

Johnny Boy dug in the toolbox for a rusty coil.

"This whole country was built on baling wire," Mr. Reeder said. "Now you can't hardly buy any new. Them chain stores in town don't carry it. This country's gone to hell since Johnny Cash died."

He began unwrapping a strand, measuring it with the length of his thumb. Mick went to the chicken house and knocked on the door.

"I'm coming in," Mick said.

He entered, leaving the door wide open to reveal Johnny Boy in the yard. Sunlight

64

spread through the interior, diffusing in the corners. Both birds were in metal cages. Roscoe lay on the couch, blinking at the sudden brightness. Mick moved swiftly through the room, lifting old clothes and pushing aside a half-empty feed sack. Beneath some movie magazines lay a nine-shot .22 revolver, an H&R on a .38 frame.

"Those are my wife's," Roscoe said.

"Gun, too?"

"No, that's mine. I meant them magazines. She don't like people messing with them."

"Roscoe," Mick said. "You need to talk to Johnny Boy. Come on outside."

"I'd rather talk to you."

"He's the deputy, not me."

"What if I don't?" Roscoe said.

"Then I'll drag you outside. Johnny Boy will cuff you and you'll be in Rocksalt talking to the sheriff."

"I didn't do nothing."

"Then come on out and talk to Johnny Boy."

"What about that castle doctrine law?"

Mick unloaded the pistol, dropped the bullets on the floor, and tossed the gun into an empty roosting box.

"There," he said. "I'm not an armed intruder. Good luck trying to tell the judge a chicken house you don't own is your castle."

Roscoe lay on the couch for a full minute in a display of defiance, then stood in a deliberately slow manner and strolled outside. His clothes were streaked with chicken manure and dried mud. He looked around, squinting against the sun.

"What do you want?" Roscoe said.

"According to your dad," Johnny Boy said, "Pete Lowe gave you a cardboard box on Wednesday."

"Yeah, he did."

"What was in the box?"

"A rooster."

"Did you buy it?"

"No," Roscoe said. "Pete wanted me to hang onto it for him."

"Why?"

"Uh, well. He had his reasons."

"You'd best tell me what they were."

"Ask Pete."

"I can't," Johnny Boy said. "Pete's dead."

Roscoe looked at Mick for confirmation. Mick nodded and Roscoe slid down the side of the chicken house as if losing strength in his legs. He sat on the concrete block that served as a step. Mick wondered how long since he'd eaten a meal and drunk water. He'd seen dehydration in the desert, and light-headedness was a sign. He resisted the impulse to offer water.

"Somebody shot him," Johnny Boy said.

"What am I supposed to do with his rooster?"

"I don't know," Johnny Boy said. "Thing is, he got killed after you seen him last. You need to tell me what's going on."

Mr. Reeder joined them, holding an oil filter wrench with a loose strap. Clamped to it was a rusty pair of vise grips intended to tighten the strap.

"Son," he said. "Where's Misty at?"

"She took off, Daddy. Been nigh a month."

"Then who's been eating all that fish?"

"Charles. Pete said to feed it to him."

"Who in the hell is Charles?" Mr. Reeder said.

"Pete Lowe's rooster," Johnny Boy said. "It's more or less why we're here. Pete's dead and your boy here is holding back. I'm trying to keep him out of the pokey."

"Hear that?" Mr. Reeder said to Roscoe. "Tell them ever what they want to know. Then you can come in and eat. I've got ham thawing. Good ham from them Amish over in Fleming County."

"I can have some?"

"Yeah, I'll make your mama's cornbread

and soup beans, too. But you got to talk to this feller."

Roscoe rubbed his head, dislodging chunks of pine shaving and straw from his hair. He looked at his father's boots as he spoke.

"Pete was afraid of Charles getting stole. He wanted me to keep him and not tell nobody."

"Why would somebody steal a rooster?" Johnny Boy said.

"It's worth three thousand dollars."

Mr. Reeder's voice took on a gentle tone.

"Son," he said. "Ain't no bird worth that much. You need to tell them the truth."

"It's true, Daddy," Roscoe said. "Charles is Mexican and German. Best fighting cock there is. He won seven times in a row."

"Where's these fights at?" Johnny Boy said.

"Different places. Usually in a barn way back in the woods."

"How do you know where to go?"

"Online chat rooms."

"When was the last fight?"

"Two weeks ago on Saturday night."

"Where was it?"

"Hack Darvis's place. On the Elliott County line."

Johnny Boy shook his head. Hack Darvis

was so crooked he screwed his britches on. Thirty years back, Hack had dropped a tree on a man while logging. People said it was deliberate, a dispute over a woman. It was just the two of them in the woods and Hack wasn't charged with a crime.

"Why'd Pete give you Charles?" Johnny Boy said.

"I just told you," Roscoe said.

"I mean why you in particular?"

"He knew I'd take care of him."

"How'd he know that?" Johnny Boy said.

"Because I got my own cock. Tiger ain't fought yet. Pete was showing me how to train him up. That's why Misty left. She said I liked Tiger more than her. Sometimes I did. Not all the time but I reckon it was enough for her to take off. That and the money."

"What money?" Johnny Boy said.

"She wanted us to rent a trailer but I bought Tiger."

The four men stood without speaking, each looking a different direction. Mick studied the woods behind the chicken house where three sparrows were taunting a crow in a sycamore. The crow stepped off a limb and began gliding. The sparrows followed, pecking at its tail feathers until the crow began flapping its wings and departed quickly. The sparrows circled back to the nest they'd protected.

Johnny Boy lifted his eyebrows to Mick and gave a slight shrug.

"Roscoe," Mick said. "Anybody else know Charles is here?"

"No."

"What about Misty?"

"She seen him when she came back for some of her stuff."

"Did you tell her whose bird it was?"

"No, Pete said not to."

"But she knew you went with him to the fights."

Roscoe nodded. Briefly all the men were nodding — Mick to Johnny Boy that he was done, Johnny Boy to Roscoe, and Mr. Reeder to his son. A blue jay yelled, then dive-bombed another jay as if playing a game. A burst of wind flipped the leaves of a silver maple.

"Mr. Reeder," Mick said. "That rooster being here is no good. One man got killed over it. If you see somebody you don't know, best call the sheriff."

"I can watch out for my boy."

"I know you can. But them people don't mess around."

In a sudden movement Mr. Reeder withdrew a snub-nose .38 from his back pocket. "I don't either," he said.

CHAPTER SIX

Linda was driving in a calm fashion, wondering why she did so. Usually she put the pedal to the metal and let it roar, following the guidance of a song she'd heard on her mother's old eight-tracks. Today she was going easy. The only difference was breakfast. Most mornings she ate a muffin on the run and got to work with half a cup of coffee in a portable thermos, already tense and anxious. Too much coffee and she got a headache. Too little and she got one, too. Today she felt in good shape — her brother's breakfast held her nervous system together while she got herself well caffeinated.

Her radio squawked twice and Sandra's voice came through.

"Base to sheriff."

"I'm here, Sandra."

"Got a call. An intruder or trespasser."

"Well, which is it?"

72

"Hard to say. It's from Mrs. Morgan, lives below Shawnee Rock. Says there's somebody there."

"Home invasion?"

"I don't know. She was a little vague. I believe she's getting up there."

"Send Johnny Boy."

"Can't. He's on the other side of the county doing that eviction."

"Damn it," Linda said. "Damn it all to hell."

The radio was silent.

"Text me the damn address," Linda said.

At the next wide spot, she turned around and headed back the way she'd come. Shawnee Rock was a natural escarpment where teenagers went to drink and smoke weed. They'd taken to spray-painting graffiti on the rock, which led to a belief that Satanists were congregating up there. Linda's subsequent investigation yielded empty beer cans, a torn hoodie, and a pack of rolling papers.

The Morgan place was at the end of a long driveway of twin ruts mounded in the middle by weeds. Trees surrounded the house below a sky the color of a mason jar. A phone line and electric wire ran from a utility pole to an old two-story house. There were no cars, which meant any intruder had come on foot. Linda got out of her vehicle and inspected the yard for footprints, finding none.

She stepped onto the porch and knocked at the door. It was freshly painted bright green, a quick and sloppy job. There was no answer and she knocked twice more, then walked around the house to check the back door. An elm grew beside the house, one of the few in the county that had survived the blight, one long limb above the roof. In the backyard was a footpath through high grass to an iron table painted white. An older woman sat at the table with a bright yellow mug and a cigarette. Her long gray hair was loose and she wore a pale housedress.

"Hold your horses," the woman said. "Who are you?"

"Sheriff Hardin."

"You're a woman."

"Yes, ma'am," Linda said. "I'm new."

Linda went closer, noticing dry flecks of green paint on the woman's right wrist.

"Paint your door?" Linda said.

"Who told you that?"

"Nobody. It looked fresh and you've still yet got a little on your arm."

"It's green," the woman said.

"I saw that."

"A green door keeps the devil away."

74

"Did you call the sheriff's office today?"

"Yes, I did. You're quick."

"I was in the area," Linda said. "What can I help you with, Mrs. Morgan?"

"Something's in the house."

"Something? You told dispatch it was a person."

"It's both."

Linda gathered a deep breath and let it out slowly, then did it twice more. It was a technique for calming that seldom worked. She was still frustrated but less likely to cuss or stomp away in frustration. Her mother had driven her nuts and Linda understood that she was vulnerable to getting irritated by older women.

"Both?" Linda said.

"It's a ghost. Used to be a person, so it's both."

"Have you seen it?"

"Twice. In the upstairs hall and on the steps."

"What'd it look like?"

"I can't rightly say. It was light gray and moving slow, then real fast."

"Do you mind if I sit down?"

Mrs. Morgan shrugged. Linda adjusted her duty belt for as much comfort as possible in the metal chair. She tilted forward in the same posture as suspects handcuffed

75

in the back seat. Mrs. Morgan's housedress had started out yellow and white, but was faded, probably from drying in the sun on the clothesline. Linda wondered if she'd glimpsed an old cloudy mirror in dim light and mistaken herself for a ghost.

"Do you have a mirror in the house?" she said.

"In the bathroom."

"Did you see the ghost in there?"

"No, I done told you. The hall and the steps. Are you not listening?"

Linda breathed deeply three times then stood.

"I think I'll look around inside," she said.

Linda crossed the yard to the back door and entered the kitchen. It was surprisingly neat, considering the woman's age and level of delusion. The surfaces had been wiped and dishes washed, dried, and stacked. A radio on the counter played a local station. She opened the refrigerator and inspected the contents. All the expiration dates were within range.

She continued into the front room, which had the same degree of tidiness. The only anomaly was the couch, where a loose stack of magazines and a pile of junk mail flanked an empty spot. Mrs. Morgan probably sat here often. Another radio played the same station as if in cut-rate stereo. The ground floor had a small sitting room and a bedroom that was clearly used by Mrs. Morgan. The bed was neatly made and the closet organized. A small radio played the same station on a table by the bed. Beside the radio was a flashlight, spare batteries for hearing aids, a box of tissue, and a paperback book about British royalty. A shiny aluminum cane with four rubber-tipped feet stood by the door.

Linda climbed the steps. A layer of dust covered each tread, none of which showed fresh footprints. The bannister was equally dusty with no handprints. At the top of the steps Linda underwent a brief fear that she would encounter a ghost in the hall. She shook her head then checked two bedrooms with slanted ceilings. Through a gabled window she could see the broad trunk of the elm. A breeze moved the leaves and she heard the scratching of the limb on the roof.

The original plaster ceiling had been patched with small panels of sheetrock, one of which was warped and stained. Linda dragged a chair to the wall and stood on it. She prodded the ceiling with a clasp of her handcuffs, then waved the cuffs in front of her face, recognizing the scent of squirrel urine.

Linda returned to the backyard. Mrs. Morgan was smoking another cigarette in a patch of sunlight. The rest of the yard was covered in shade from the massive stone outcrop behind the house.

"Well," Linda said, "I've figured out your problem. You've got squirrels in the eaves. And a tree branch scrapes the roof. It might stir the squirrels up, you know, get them rattled."

"I know about the squirrels. Did you see the ghost?"

"No, I didn't," Linda said. "What's it look like?"

"It's a man hunting his gun."

"Do you have a gun in the house?"

"I did, but not no more. My nephew borrowed it twenty-some years ago. Never brought it back. It was my great-granddaddy's twenty-two rifle. He used it on small game."

"Uh-huh," Linda said. "What makes you think this ghost is after a gun?"

"You're not from around here, are you?"

"I've lived in Eldridge County all my life."

"Rocksalt, I reckon."

"Yes, ma'am."

The woman used her cigarette as a pointer and gestured to the dark cliff beyond the yard.

"Do you know what that is?" she said.

"I'd say it's the back side of Shawnee Rock."

"You've been towned so long, you forgot the country. Shawnee Rock is haunted. Folks hereabouts know that. There's three ghosts living up there."

"Three?"

"A baby looking for its head. A bear looking for its hide. And a man hunting for his gun. He shot the bear that killed his baby, then dropped his gun. He's in my house hunting for it."

"Why would he do that?"

"Because he can't find it up there."

Mrs. Morgan's tone held an element of frustration as if she were explaining the fundamentals of arithmetic to a child who wasn't paying attention. Linda considered the existence of ghosts to be possible but she'd never seen one. Empirical evidence rarely mattered — most people hadn't seen the devil but they still painted their front doors green. She supposed it was the same with UFOs, Bigfoot, and Santa Claus. Linda still recalled the crushing disappointment upon learning that the tooth fairy was her mom.

"Mrs. Morgan," Linda said. "If there's three ghosts on Shawnee Rock, any one of them might have come down here."

"The baby, it can't walk on account of being a baby. That bear got itself gutted on the Rock, so it'll stay close to its hide. The man, he lost his gun down the cliff. My opinion, he's looked all up and down this holler and didn't find it. That leaves my house."

Linda admired the woman's impeccable logic. She'd reasoned through options in the same fashion that Linda ruled out suspects. Linda shifted in the chair. The heavy woods enclosed the yard in walls of green. A flicker with a red cap walked headfirst down a shagbark hickory, found a soft spot in the bark, and used its beak like a miniature jackhammer. Linda wondered if a tree could be haunted by a dead bug. If so, the entire woods would be filled with more ghosts than insects.

She wasn't sure how to proceed with Mrs. Morgan. Briefly she wondered if her brother had seen the ghosts of soldiers on battle-grounds. For all Mick's hardened ways, he was good-hearted and she tried to think what he might do in her situation. He'd want to reassure Mrs. Morgan, relieve her anxiety, then move on. Effective in the short term, the strategy had eventually ruined his marriage. Still, Linda had never been married, so what did she know about preserving one?

Mrs. Morgan lit another cigarette.

"Does somebody bring you food and cigarettes?" Linda said.

"My nephew."

"The one with your gun?"

"Yes, he comes by twice a week. Helps pay all my bills, too. Runs me to the doctors."

"He give you that cane in your bedroom?"

"Yes, but I don't need it."

"Did you tell him about the ghost?"

"No. I ain't about to, either. He'd throw me in a home."

"What about moving in with your nephew?"

"He's on his second wife with five kids. Thank you, no."

Linda nodded, thinking things through. Mrs. Morgan was taking care of the house. Her clothes and hair were clean. She wasn't completely alone, just lonely. Linda leaned forward and looked at the woman, letting her know they were getting down to business.

"What would you like me to do?" Linda said.

"What do you mean?"

"You called the sheriff and here I am."

"I don't know," Mrs. Morgan said. "I got tired of the ghost and figured the law was who to tell."

"I could arrest him. You'd have to press charges. There'll be paperwork but I don't think it'd go to court."

"I wouldn't testify if it did. Shoot, my nephew'd have me in the crazy house. I've never lived anywhere but here."

"How about this?" Linda said. "I'll take the ghost in custody and give him a talking-to. I'll tell him to leave the county or go to jail."

"Think he'll listen?"

"He won't have a choice, Mrs. Morgan. I'm the law."

Linda stood and adjusted her belt. She went in the house and climbed the steps to the hall. Mrs. Morgan waited downstairs.

"Sir," Linda said loud enough for Mrs. Morgan to hear. "Sir, you need to come with me."

She stared at a blank wall for a few seconds, then moved to the top of the steps. She raised her left arm perpendicular to her body and cupped her hand as if holding someone by the upper arm. She descended slowly, speaking loud.

"Sir, this isn't your home. You need to stay away from this house. If I have to come back again, it'll go a whole lot worse. Don't be coming around here no more."

She walked past Mrs. Morgan, whose eyes were intense with concentration. Linda went outside and crossed the front yard to her vehicle. She opened the rear door and pantomimed helping someone in, placing her hand where their head would be to make sure it didn't get bumped. She closed the door and went back to the house.

Mrs. Morgan stood on the porch, her slim arms around her chest. The faded house-dress swayed in the breeze below her knees.

"That'll do it," Linda said.

"I don't want anything to happen to him."

"I guarantee you he won't go to jail."

"It's not his fault," Mrs. Morgan said. "He can't help it, I don't reckon."

"I understand."

"I'm glad you do because I don't exactly. I just go along with these old hills."

"That's all any of us can do."

Linda got in her car, turned around, and drove back down the narrow lane. She glanced in the rearview mirror instinctively. The back seat was vacant and she grinned to herself. She notified Sandra that the intruder was a false alarm and there'd be no report. She headed further east, deeper into the hills, thinking that Mrs. Morgan

83

was a lonely old woman on her own. The way things were going in Linda's life, she'd be in the same boat one day. A little kindness never hurt.

CHAPTER SEVEN

Johnny Boy and Mick drove out the ridge from the Reeders' and stopped at the top of the hill. Johnny Boy called Linda but got no answer. He left a message then radioed dispatch.

"Sandra," he said. "Where's Linda at? She's not answering."

"Other side of Shawnee Rock. There's no reception up there."

"Tell her I need to talk to her."

"Ten-four," Sandra said.

"Copy that."

"Over and out."

He grinned and released the radio button. Mick understood that this was Johnny Boy's way of flirting. They drove down the hill, swerving around dried-up mud holes. Johnny Boy stopped for a box turtle. Mick left the truck and carried it to safety, remembering that as a boy he'd painted a big red X on every turtle he found, hoping

85

to see it again. He never had. Maybe the paint faded from weather or maybe there was a secret colony of red-tinted turtles deep in the woods. He returned to the truck, where Johnny Boy was filling Linda in on the Reeders.

"Yeah, he's here," Johnny Boy said. "Okay."

He put the phone on speaker. Mick heard his sister's tinny voice, sounding harried and under pressure. The reception slid in and out as if she were in a tunnel.

"Go see Hack Darvis," she said.

"All right," Johnny Boy said. "You want me to bring him in for running a cockfight?"

"No, we got bigger fish to fry than two birds fighting. Tell him —"

The call ended abruptly. Johnny Boy tried twice to reconnect, with no luck. A large green katydid flew through the open window and landed on the dashboard. Startled, Johnny Boy dropped the phone in his lap. Mick plucked the insect between his fingers and released it outside.

"One of my two favorite bugs," Mick said. "They camouflage as a leaf. My papaw counted the number of chirps they made in fifteen seconds then added thirty-seven to know the temperature of the air."

"My family used a thermometer."

Mick nodded, thinking of his mother's twelve thermometers. He'd never used either method but simply stepped outside to gauge whether he needed a jacket.

"Thing is," Johnny Boy said, "that technique only works when it's between forty and seventy. Any hotter and you can't count fast enough. If the temperature is below thirty-eight, there wouldn't be any sound."

"I guess you're better at math than my papaw was."

"What's your other favorite insect? You said you had two."

"Stick bug. It's hard to spot."

"Adam must have been tired that day. Naming a bug a stick bug because it looks like a stick. You ever think about Adam?"

"Never did."

"I have," Johnny Boy said. "Hours of it. Every word Adam said was the name of something. You can tell when he ran out of steam. Like the fly. He was wore out that day. Saw a little bug flying and said, 'That's a fly.' He had a tough life."

"How so?"

"Lived alone with no friends and had to give everything a name. Finally got a woman and ran into trouble over food. Then they got evicted from their home. One of their boys killed the other and ran off. I think

87

about how sad that was for them. Thrown out of paradise with a murderer for a son."

"Uh-huh," Mick said. "You need to ask dispatch for Hack's address."

Johnny Boy radioed Sandra and Mick left the truck to avoid listening to the feeble flirting. He wondered if he was jealous. He didn't think so but he wasn't thinking at a full throttle, hadn't been since leaving the base. His grandfather said that seeing a stick bug was good luck. He also said killing a daddy longlegs would make it rain and a bird in the house meant someone would die. Eventually both came true — rain fell and people died.

Mick got in the truck and they drove to the blacktop. Johnny Boy took Open Fork Road up another hill. They passed a cemetery, several trailers, and a few older homes built of wood. The terrain of the hills was so rugged that roads followed creeks, which gave the roads their names. Lick Fork Creek split to Upper Lick Fork and Lower Lick Fork. All these designations made sense to Mick except "Open Fork." Weren't all forks more or less open? A closed fork was a dead-end road or a single chopstick.

They followed Christy Creek into old Hoggtown, then deeper into the steep hills toward Elliott County. The road was draped with the low branches of maple trees.

"You think this killing's over chickens?" Johnny Boy said.

"I don't know. Depends on how much money is in it."

"Could be something inside a rooster."

"What do you mean?"

"On TV I seen a movie about a goose. Old-time black-and-white one. The show, I mean, not the goose, but it was black and white, too. Somebody stole a diamond and fed it to a Christmas goose. He lost the goose and went looking for it all over town."

"I believe a diamond would kill these little banty birds."

"The goose on TV died, too."

The land opened to a broad, flat area tucked beneath the lip of the hills, one of those strange geographic anomalies of the region. It was a large oval the size of a high school running track. One side was bordered by the limestone cliffs of the ridge above. The other side fell away steeply, rain gullies twining down the heavily wooded slope. They passed a cleared field of matted grass filled with tire tracks and ruts, a makeshift parking lot. A single post held a floodlight with wires that ran to a barn and two outbuildings. Parked in front was an extended-cab pickup and a Ford Galaxie

500 with stacked headlights.

Johnny Boy stopped and blew the horn three times. He waited two minutes and honked again. The noise lingered in the air, slowly fading until the only sound was wind brushing the high boughs.

Mick left the vehicle, watching three buzzards circle at different altitudes, slowly descending as if each had been assigned a thermal. The truck keys were in the ignition. The glove box held official registration in the name of Hack Darvis.

The barn door was the massive kind that slid on a box rail bolted to the front. Johnny Boy gripped the handle and moved it easily on the greased track, allowing sunlight to drench the interior. It was empty of standard equipment stored in a barn — no tractor, tiller, or even hay. The center held a broad hole, twelve feet across and six inches deep. The dirt was packed down along the edges with boot prints visible. In the center of the ring the earth was churned and loose, mixed with feathers and dried blood. It smelled of slaughter, whiskey, and cigarettes.

Lengths of lumber lying across concrete blocks served as a crude form of bleachers. A cattle stall had a shelf built into the half door. Strewn about the hard dirt inside lay empty cardboard boxes emblazoned with the names of cheap liquor. Another stall held scrap lumber. The rest of the barn was empty except for crushed beer cans and hundreds of cigarette butts.

"Heck of an operation," Johnny Boy said.

They went outside. Two sheds were locked and Mick removed the keys from the truck's ignition. Mick went to the first shed and tried three keys before opening the padlock. He entered, flicked the switch by the door, and a bare light bulb came on overhead. A workbench held six cases of warm beer. Beside it were two boxes filled with half-pints of cheap whiskey.

The other shed had no windows, a new roof of corrugated steel, and a heavy door with concealed hinges and two padlocks. Mick opened them and went inside. There was a small refrigerator and a low table on which sat a quart jar, a sponge, a long plastic tube, and a box of cling wrap. The refrigerator contained a capped jar and two spoons. The thermostat was set surprisingly low considering the lack of perishables. Hanging from the wall was a pair of thick leather welding gloves and a long metal rod with a blunt hook at one end.

On a table lay a heavy wooden box hinged like a suitcase, well built for rough use, reminding Mick of a supply case for an oil painter who worked outdoors. Mick slid the bolt lock free, released the hasps, and opened the box. A loud buzzing filled the air. In the box lay a coiled rattlesnake with the tip of its tail upraised and vibrating. A thick screen formed a barrier to cage the snake but Mick leaped backward instinctively. He'd experienced close-quarters combat in three countries but the only thing that filled him with instant terror was a rattlesnake, a fear instilled in him as a child. He pulled the metal rod from the wall and used it to flip the snake box shut, then ran the bolt to lock it. The buzzing became muffled.

Johnny Boy held his gun in a two-handed stance aimed at the box.

"Put that away," Mick said.

Johnny Boy lowered the gun.

"Don't ever draw a weapon when I'm standing in front of you again. You hear me?"

"I don't like snakes."

"I don't like getting shot."

They went outside, both grateful for the sun and air. The landscape lay green and bright around them as if nothing else mattered. A butterfly flitted among honeysuckle at the edge of the woods.

"How big you think that snake was?"

Johnny Boy said.

"Two feet at least. That box looked made for it. Maybe he's some kind of Pentecostal."

"None here in Eldridge County. I mean there's Pentecostals that talk in tongues but not snake handlers. They got a Holiness Church over in Pick County that used to fool with them. It's legal if it's a family church."

"You know any of them?"

"No, but I got a cousin who sells them snakes."

Two more buzzards circled in the sky above the barn. A billowy cloud drifted behind their black shapes. Johnny Boy watched them.

"Must be looking for dead roosters."

Mick nodded, thinking that something wasn't right. Nothing he could name but he'd learned to trust his instincts in Iraq and Afghanistan. His gun was back at the sheriff's station and he didn't like being without it. They walked behind the barn, where an ATV was parked at the top of a trail that dropped to the holler. Perched on the ATV's roll cage was a crow watching two buzzards dig their featherless heads into a dead man. Johnny Boy turned away and gagged.

"Go call Linda," Mick said. "Get an ambulance."

Gasping for breath, Johnny Boy climbed the hill, holding his phone up, seeking reception. Mick yelled and charged the birds. They lifted awkwardly from the ground and landed in a hickory, staring as if in reproach at the interruption of their meal. Mick didn't mind. They had their job, same as him, and he wouldn't judge an animal for its work, even if it was eating carrion.

The body was that of a big man, tall and broad, lying askew in the dirt. A nine-millimeter Glock lay near one hand. His shirt and pants were shredded from buckshot that had chopped out a big enough chunk of his torso to kill him. Mick turned in a tight circle, studying the land, sight-lines, and the proximity of the barn to the ATV. The man had been shot at close range. Someone had followed him or they'd both come back here together. Maybe the killer was waiting for him.

Mick stepped into the cool shade of a maple. He sat on the ground between two roots rising from the earth and leaned against the tree trunk, feeling more comfortable than he had in weeks. Maybe it was being at a crime scene. He wondered if it was a mistake to leave the army. A cardinal flashed red in a crabapple tree. He didn't miss the army, he'd missed sitting in the woods he'd grown up in. It was the only place he'd ever felt safe.

CHAPTER EIGHT

Linda hit a rare straight stretch in the hills.
Like all country drivers she steered to the
center of the blacktop and floored the accelerator. Compelled to slow by a curve,
she occupied herself by mentally reviewing
what she knew about the death of Pete
Lowe, which was pretty much nothing.
Three days earlier, she'd examined the
crime scene after it was trampled by EMTs,
the county medical examiner, and three
neighbors. Hadn't any of them ever seen a
cop show on TV?

Pete Lowe had five kids, four of whom had
married and moved out of the county. The
oldest daughter, Janice, had found the body,
and called 911. Linda had tried to interview
her but the funeral had interfered. She left
the blacktop for a gravel road that gradually
became dirt as it followed a creek up a holler. Twice Linda drove through the shallow
water that crossed the road. The road ended

at a yellow house with new shingles. Linda parked, honked, and stood beside the vehicle. The air was still, half the land in shadow from the high hills on both sides. Full sun would last a few hours per day. In winter, it would be a gray place but well sheltered from wind and weather.

A woman wearing a denim barn coat and rubber boots stepped around the house. Her hair was tucked beneath a blue-and-white cap bearing the emblem of Tractor Supply. Mud spattered her clothes.

"Mrs. Moore?" Linda said. "Janice Moore?"

"Yes and no. I'm divorced so it's Miss and I'm back to being a Lowe."

"You're Pete's daughter?"

Janice nodded.

"I'm sorry about your daddy," Linda said. "I'd like to talk if you've got a minute."

"Uh . . . Well. I'm in the middle of something."

"I can wait or I can give you a hand."

"Up to you."

Janice turned and walked around the house. Linda followed her to a penned lot made of T-posts and hog wire. A trough built from two-by-eights ran along the fence on the side nearest to the house. In the center of the muddy lot stood a galvanized tank of water. Two young sows lay in the mud. A mature boar stood parallel to the fence with one back leg tied to a post. Around his neck was a rope that held his head snug against another post. Janice squatted outside the fence beside the hog. Careful to stay clear of its sharp teeth, she lashed its front leg to the fence, stood, and gestured to a broken hoe handle on the grass.

"It's pretty much a one-person job," Janice said. "If a rope breaks, beat on him until I get out."

Linda picked up the hickory handle, watching Janice push the top of the fence down with one hand. She swung a leg over, planted her boot firmly in the mud, and crossed the wire. The hog strained, rattling the fence, startling four sparrows from a maple. From her pocket Janice withdrew a small bottle of rubbing alcohol, uncapped it, and lodged it in the wet earth. She squatted behind the hog. The hog kicked backward with its free leg but lost its balance and tipped toward the fence. It kicked several times then stopped to rest.

"Get ready," Janice said to Linda. "Hit him in the head if you have to. Won't hurt him. They've got a hard skull. But it'll get his attention off me."

Janice opened a pocketknife and doused it with alcohol. She reached between the hog's legs and cupped its scrotum. Holding it with one hand, she cut a two-inch slit in the skin, squeezed out one testicle, sliced it free, and slipped it in her coat pocket. The hog was screaming like a child and slamming its huge body against the fence. Janice made another incision and removed the second testicle. The hog screamed with greater ferocity. Janice crossed the fence and cut the ropes. The hog ran wildly around the lot, still shrieking, slinging muck in the air. It entered a shelter in the far corner and lapsed into moaning.

Janice offered a testicle to Linda. It was gray and pink, flecked with pocket lint.

"Want one?" Janice said. "Fry them up. Good for iron and zinc."

"I'm all right, thanks."

Janice cleaned blood from the knife and her hands. The air had stilled after the melee until a chickadee gave a tentative call. A crow watched from a birch as if waiting for its chance to scout the entrails.

"Will that hog be all right?" Linda said.

"Yeah. It's better to do it when they're young but I just got this one."

"You raise hogs?"

"Here lately, yes. I help people with their

animals. Unofficial veterinarian. If they don't have money, they pay me different ways. That's how I got them."

"Where'd you learn to do it?"

"Army. Medical training. If you can doctor a human you can doctor a dog or cow. Animals are harder. You can't explain things to them."

"Some people are the same way."

Janice laughed, then stopped as if the sound was abruptly corked. She used the back of the knife to scrape mud from her sleeves, flinging it to the earth.

"Find out anything about Daddy?" she said.

"I'm doing my best. Were y'all close?"

"Not really. Too much alike. I went by a couple of times a week, dropping off food mainly."

"Did he mention any trouble?"

"No, but he wouldn't. He didn't like me fussing over him, didn't want to be a burden. I mean, he appreciated the meals I brought, but didn't like that I did it. He was stubbed up that way."

"We couldn't find his cell phone."

"He didn't have one."

"Are you sure? There was a regular phone in the house but it was disconnected."

"He didn't pay the bill on it. Said if

anybody wanted to talk to him, they could drive up there and find him. I guess somebody did."

Janice wiped the blade of the pocketknife on her sleeve, folded it, and tucked it away. She walked along the fence, testing its strength to see if the hog's wild flailing had loosened the wire.

"Wanted to ask you something," Linda said. "There was a chicken coop at his house and half a bag of new straw. But no chickens. I wondered what happened to them."

"He loved those chickens. Had eight laying hens. He named them every one — Popsicle, Bathtub, Flora, Vera, Strawberry Head. I forgot the others. A fox killed them. He was tore up about it. Then he got a rooster, a little one. I thought it was funny, a rooster with no hens, but it cheered him up. He took care of that thing like it was a show horse. I figured he was making up for the hens getting killed. Pampering it."

"We didn't find the rooster."

"You think somebody stole it?"

"I don't know what to think," Linda said. "I'm trying to understand things is all. Do you own a shotgun?"

"I don't own any guns."

"You know anybody mad at your daddy?"

"We didn't talk about stuff like that. He worked on race cars. Them fellers might know more."

"Any women in his life?"

"No. Mom died and he gave up on most things. What he was, was a sad man who lived alone with his birds."

Linda nodded, thanked her, and walked back to her car. At the corner of the house she turned to wave but Janice was gone. It occurred to Linda that Janice was a sad woman who lived alone with her hogs.

Linda drove to the main road and radioed Sandra that she was heading for Leo Gowan's house, the nearest neighbor to Pete. While driving, she thought about a date at a restaurant in Lexington that served lamb fries. The man, Barton or Bert, something like that, insisted on driving his Humvee, which he was inordinately proud of. Linda despised it. The height from the ground, its absurd ostentatiousness, but most of all the quality of the ride itself — loud, jarring, and slow. Her back hurt like a toothache by the time they arrived at the restaurant. Lamb fries turned out to be sheep testicles, sliced, battered, and deep-fried. She took two small bites out of politeness. Her date — Bateman, she suddenly remembered — ate three servings and finished hers while regaling Linda with stories of Rocky Mountain oysters he'd consumed at a festival in Montana. He showed her proof on his phone — a photo of him holding a beer and wearing a T-shirt with the slogan I HAD A BALL! He explained that eating bull testicles made him more virile and suggested a nightcap at a motel bar nearby. Linda agreed. While he parked the absurd vehicle, a prolonged undertaking due to its wide turning radius, Linda went to the motel lobby, called a cab, and arranged to meet it at a Waffle House two blocks away. The taxi fare to Rocksalt was $190. It took two months to eradicate it from her credit card but she didn't mind — every nickel was worth it.

Linda had always known she was smarter than most men, which wasn't really saying a lot about a group of people who believed eating animal balls improved their sex lives. Men were morons who abused women and killed each other. Linda couldn't figure out why she liked them. Maybe she didn't but just got lonely.

The onboard GPS directed her to a T-intersection but gave no instructions on which way to turn. The address wasn't on the grid. Technology had given up. She took a left and went a few miles, vigilant for any turnoff, then turned around and went the other way. Twenty minutes later she saw a mailbox partially concealed by the white blossoms of a mountain camellia. She followed a dirt road along a rain gully that ran off the hill. The road veered east to a steep incline with a wide spot at the base. She stopped, left the car, and gauged the ruts. It was dry enough to drive in low gear. Linda engaged the four-wheel drive and began a slow ascent. Sunlight dappled the dirt road with the shadows of leaves like a shifting kaleidoscope. At the top, the road made a hard turn along a narrow ridge that had been cleared of trees and brush. A GMC 4×4 was parked in front of a small house. Beside it was a Ford Fusion. Both had Eldridge County plates.

Linda stopped and confirmed her location with dispatch. The connection was weak, filled with static, but she figured the general idea would get through. She stepped from the SUV and waited in case the Gowans had dogs. She'd had to mace two in the past, acts she'd felt terrible about, worse than having to club a drunk man trying to fight. The only sound was wind rustling leaves in the upper boughs of the trees that surrounded her. She approached the house, intending to stop twenty feet away and yell.

From within came shouting, a man and a woman, their voices increasing in volume. Linda stopped, waiting for the argument to end or one of them to leave the house. Instead, she heard the sharp sound of a large caliber gunshot. She began running to the house, hand on her duty holster to deactivate the retention device. A child screamed inside the house and Linda drew her sidearm, ran up the steps, and pushed the door open. Another gunshot roared in the confined quarters and she was aware of a terrible pain. She stumbled against the doorjamb. A lightning bolt ran from her legs to her chest. She felt weak and tried to hold onto her weapon. She couldn't see well and didn't know if the house was dimly lit or if her vision was slipping. As if from a great distance she heard the sound of a loud thump and realized she'd fallen.

Linda understood she'd been shot and knew if the bullet had hit an artery she'd bleed to death in minutes. She needed to get to her car. She pushed herself to her knees, grimacing at the pain, and began crawling out the door. The Ford Fusion was driving away. She wanted to yell after it but needed to conserve her strength for the long crawl to her vehicle.

CHAPTER NINE

Two buzzards crouched in a low branch watching Mick, occasionally cocking their heads to monitor any competition for the body of Hack Darvis. Mick threw a rock that struck the branch. He grinned when the birds lifted their wings, flew in a wide circle, and perched on a tree a few feet away. He'd deliberately aimed at the limb, not the buzzards, preferring to frighten them off instead of hurting them.

As a kid Mick had spent hundreds of hours developing the skill of throwing a rock. The main thing was choice of rock — as evenly weighted as possible with no protuberances that would catch air and cause it to swerve. Golf-ball size was ideal for his small hands. For a while he'd used rocks to hunt squirrels with minor success. When his grandfather learned about the undertaking, he taught Mick how to shoot a .22 rifle. Range and accuracy were better, but if he missed, the sound scared the squirrel away. At nine years old, he preferred rocks.

A third buzzard arrived, landing on the yellow-clay dirt and ruffling its feathers. It took two steps toward the body, then flapped back into the air at the blast of a car horn. The other birds departed and Mick stood. The horn came in a steady series of short-short-short, then long-long-long, and Mick recognized the Morse code. He hurried up the slope. Johnny Boy was driving fast down the dirt road, still using the horn. He stopped and gestured to Mick.

"Linda got shot," Johnny Boy said.

"How bad?"

"I don't know. Ambulance is on the way."

"Shit."

"She'll be at the hospital by the time we get there. Come on."

"No," Mick said. "I'll take your car."

"We should both go."

"This is a crime scene. You're the sheriff now. You have to stay."

Mick opened the driver-side door and Johnny Boy stepped out, suddenly overwhelmed by responsibility. Mick spun the car in a tight circle and sped away. The sound of the car engine faded, replaced by songbirds.

Johnny Boy nodded to himself, took a breath, squared his shoulders, and went around the house and down the slope. Three buzzards surrounded the body. One took a tentative peck at the dead man's leg just above the boot. Johnny Boy withdrew his sidearm and fired for the first time as a law officer. All three birds leaped awkwardly into flight and vanished in the sky. Johnny Boy holstered his pistol and looked around. He didn't have transportation or radio contact. He was his own backup and he'd missed shooting a large bird at close range. He was off to a bad start as sheriff.

A faint path went down the hill, wide enough for an ATV, but he saw no sign of recent tread marks. Visible in a patch of dirt was the edge of a footprint. At the bottom of the slope was a dry creek with fine dirt on the edges, then a layer of small rock. The footprints were distinct in the soft earth and Johnny Boy photographed each one. He crossed the creek bed to a narrow path that ended at a dirt road. The footprints stopped at the road beside a set of tire tracks. The vehicle had come down the road from the north, then turned around and gone back the same way. Johnny Boy photographed the tire tread from various angles, getting close-ups of the deepest tracks. He found an intact print of a shoe with part of a brand name and a size — Iris 7 — and photographed it several times.

The tire tracks went up the hill and stopped where a tree blown down by wind had blocked the trail. Somebody had chainsawed two sections from the tree to make room for the vehicle's passage. The sawdust was damp but still yellowish, meaning a few days old. Johnny Boy photographed the sawdust and cut logs. He went back down the hill, crossed the creek, and climbed to Hack's place, walking slowly along the edge of the path. He was glad to be alone, that no one had witnessed his first act as a sheriff — shooting his service weapon at birds. He felt miserable. There was nothing to do but wait for Marquis Sledge, the county coroner.

With great reluctance he returned to the shed and found short pieces of rope and a long leather strip of old harness. The rattlesnake box had two clasps that were locked tight but he bound it anyway, his hands gentle as if handling eggs or an infant. From inside came a dull thump, but no buzzing of rattles. Anxiety tightened his chest. He felt hollow and distant. But he was sheriff now, no two ways about it, and the snake was evidence. Evidence of what, he didn't know, but it was his job to secure the scene, and preside over the body. He set the box on the table and went outside to wait.

CHAPTER TEN

Mick drove to town with the light bar flashing. Two cars pulled over for him and he nearly clipped a slow-moving truck pulling a cattle trailer. In Rocksalt he ran two red lights, entered the hospital parking lot, and parked by the double doors of the emergency entrance. He hurried to the plexiglass intake window.

"Linda Hardin," he said. "I'm her brother."

"She's in ICU."

"How bad?"

"Critical. That's all I know. Please have a seat. The doctor will talk to you when he's finished."

Mick paced briefly then sat to conserve energy. The chair was institutionally comfortable, which meant better than all military furniture. Across from him was a man dozing. A woman with an infant stared into space as if seeing another dimension where she wasn't waiting fearfully in a hospital.

The sliding door to the parking lot opened and in walked two men — Rocksalt police chief Chet Logan and the new mayor, Larry Slocum. Mick nodded to them. He'd gone to high school with the chief, who walked with a slight limp from a gunshot wound to his hip ten years back. In an odd way, it had boosted his career. Unable to perform field duty, he'd flourished behind the desk and recently been promoted to chief.

"How is she?" Chet said.

"I don't know. She's still in there. They won't tell me nothing."

"They will me."

Chet bypassed the intake window and walked down the hall to the nurses station. The mayor owned a car dealership and had the perpetual manner of a small-town salesman, eager for small talk that would initiate the thinnest of short-term social bonding. Aside from the high school principal, he was the only man in town who always wore a sport coat.

"How you holding up?" the mayor said.

Mick ignored him. That kind of cliché question always irritated him. It didn't really require an answer because it was only asked when someone was under duress. The polite response was "Hanging in there" or some

112

equally moronic cliché. It was like approaching the only survivor of an airplane crash and asking if they were okay.

"She'll make it," the mayor said. "She's got a lot of gizzard."

"You know her?"

"Yeah, we dated back before I got married."

Mick nodded. His sister had dated all the eligible men in Eldridge County. A lot of them were one-date lunkheads and he wondered if the mayor was one. Despair washed over him, a familiar feeling that he banished immediately.

The police chief walked slowly back to the waiting area, face stoic.

"She'll live," he said. "Another five minutes and she'd have bled out."

"Is she stable?" Mick said.

"Still critical. They moved her to the OR. Doc said there's extensive tissue damage from a gunshot wound to the left tibia. It'll need external fixators."

"What?" the mayor said.

"Shinbone and pins," Mick said. "Can they save the leg?"

"There's an osteopathic surgeon in there now," Chet said. "Amputation below the knee is possible. If that's the case, they'll airlift her to Lexington. Chopper's on

113

standby."

"They got a bone man here?"

"Yeah. He was on a weekly visit when Linda came in. Lucky."

Mick nodded. Luck always worked both ways. Your roof could blow off in a tornado and the neighbors would say you were lucky not to lose more. It was easy to be optimistic about other people's woes.

"Who's working the scene?" Mick said.

"I sent a man to assist Johnny Boy."

"Johnny Boy's not there. He's at Hack Darvis's place. Hack's dead. Looks like a shotgun. Johnny Boy can't do both."

"I'll get a man to Hack's, too."

The chief left, pulling his phone from a pocket as he stepped outside. The mayor hopped from his seat as if yanked by invisible rope.

"I'll call the state police," he said. "Hang in there, Mick. Those prosthetic legs they got now are good as gold. My nephew's got one. It's like a curved spring and fits in a boot. He can run a footrace with it."

The mayor left and Mick was grateful for the privacy. He'd been in this position a dozen times — waiting for medical information about wounded personnel — but never for a member of his family. A sudden fear of losing Linda chilled him to the marrow.

He pushed the sensation aside and boxed it in. It was out of his hands. He'd treat her shooting like any other case.

Linda had been interviewing Pete Lowe's neighbors, which increased the possibility that her getting shot was related to his murder. But Pete Lowe and Hack Darvis had been killed by a shotgun at close range. Why would the killer change weapons to shoot Linda? Maybe he disposed of the shotgun. Or maybe he carried multiple weapons. One thing for sure — the guy was an amateur and Mick was a professional. He'd track the man down. If Linda died, so would her killer. If she lost her leg, Mick would shoot his kneecap off.

He shook his head rapidly to rid himself of such thoughts. Anger focused his mind, fury would propel action, but wrath was a trap that created mistakes. He told the intake attendant he was going outside. She asked for his cell number and he realized the phone was in his truck at the sheriff's office.

Chet sat in his patrol car, one hand holding the onboard microphone, the other his cell phone. He was nodding and talking to one then the other. Dusk had settled over the western hills, transforming the trees into dark shapes of velour. The air was calm in the narrow valley that surrounded town. Two men smoked cigarettes beside a truck. Chet opened his door, swiveled on the car seat carefully, and placed both feet on the asphalt in order to stand. Mick watched, hoping his sister wouldn't have to learn to do the same.

"How is she?" Chet said.

"No change a minute ago."

"Something you need to know. The house where she was, there's a body there. A man. Shot through the lungs."

"She get one in him?"

"Too soon to know. They found her service weapon. Can't tell if it's been fired or how many times."

"Blood on it?"

"Yeah."

"Good. Means she had it out when she got shot. You ID the body?"

"Name of Leo Gowan. It's his house. Think your sister knew him?"

"I don't know. She was looking into Pete Lowe's murder."

"What the hell is going on, Mick? We got three dead men and a shot sheriff."

"No idea," he said. "I need to get back in there."

They walked to the entrance, Mick moving slowly to accommodate Chet's gait of swinging his bad leg a little wide with every step.

"Don't worry," Chet said. "This is from getting shot in the hip. She'll be able to walk fine."

"What's the mayor doing here anyhow?"

"Oh, he's got to poke his nose in everything in case the press shows up. The *Rock-salt News* shut down but he does it anyway."

"Can I borrow your cell phone a minute?"

Chet passed it over. Mick called Raymond and asked him to bring his truck to the hospital. Raymond listened, grunted, and hung up. In the waiting room the mayor was talking to three people with dazed expressions on their faces. He spun to Mick and Chet.

"Good news," he said. "They saved the leg. She's staying here."

"Surgery?" Mick said.

"Excuse me a minute," the mayor said.

He moved away, running three fingers through his hair as a makeshift comb, then tugged his trousers to his waist. Parked in front of the ER door was a van for the Action News team out of Lexington. A camera operator checked his equipment while a young reporter was busy squaring her shoulders and adjusting her lapels.

"How'd they get here so fast?" Mick said.

"It's been an hour and a half," Chet said. "My guess is the mayor called them."

"I've lost my sense of time. Seems like three minutes. That never happened before."

"Your sister never got shot before, either. I'm going to the scene. Could be a long surgery. You need to rest if you can."

Mick nodded. Chet left, moving with determination across the scuffed tile floor. A commotion arose from one corner of the waiting room. A doctor in scrubs was giving good news to an exhausted family of eight. Mick sensed their relief. Briefly he hoped for the same but had learned the futility of hope in the desert. It sustained people when they were powerless — incarcerated, wounded, or trapped. Hope was a desire for something to change in the future, circumstances beyond one's control. Mick saw hope as the flip side of despair, another mental state to avoid, another lesson of war.

He shook his head rapidly and went outside to the parking lot. A lone starling perched in a Japanese maple growing from an island of grass. He watched the bird, saying hello in his mind. Did the bird hope for a worm? No, it remained vigilant to food and threat. If anything gave Mick hope, it was birds, their hollow-boned flight and imperviousness to weather.

He saw his truck enter the lot. Raymond got out and came his way holding a box of food and Mick's cell phone.

"How is she?" Raymond said.

"Surgery."

Mick took the phone and checked his messages — none. In the past he'd have been grateful for the absence but now it left him bereft. Still, Raymond was standing before him and Linda was under the knife. She'd be all right. Mick dropped the gate of his truck bed. Raymond sat with him as he ate three tacos, legs dangling off the back like a kid on a bench.

What Mick wanted was bourbon, the best method of coping with stress, and the absolute worst as well. It'd been a long time since he drank and he could imagine the first shot numbing his mouth, warming his torso, and firing jolts of electricity down his legs that bounced off his feet and back up to his chest. It was a remarkable feeling, among the best. Then he'd try to relive it with another shot, then another, and another until the bottle was gone and he'd regret not buying two bottles. He loved it, which was why he tried not to drink. On a practical level, a hospital was the worst place to be drunk. But then, where was the best? Alone in the woods at night. A small fire, a camp chair, two bottles, and nothing to do the next day.

Mick and Raymond went inside and sat in a far corner of the waiting room away from other people. Two hours passed. Raymond dozed, following the Marine dictum of rest when you can. Mick shut his mind off. He'd learned the technique on long troop flights, then overnight bivouacs in preparation for attack. It was a kind of active repose that made time flow faster and reduced the anxiety and fear. The key was to breathe slowly, with the exhale longer than the inhale.

Johnny Boy arrived, boots muddy, face drawn and exhausted.

"Any news?" he said.

Mick shook his head. Johnny Boy went to the intake window. Mick could hear his voice, urgent and tense. A few minutes later he returned and sat heavily in a chair that was fastened to another one. Mick wondered vaguely if it was for security — if you stole one, you had to steal both.

"She's out of the worst part," Johnny Boy said. "They'll work on her another couple of hours, then move her to a room. Under sedation for at least four hours after that. Nothing to do but wait."

"Thanks," Mick said. "Anything at the scene?"

"I didn't go yet. Came here after Marquis pronounced Hack and did whatever it is he does. Down the hill behind the barn were footprints and tire tracks. I think somebody parked down there, came up, and shot Hack."

"Chet's at the Gowan house. Said they found a man dead."

"I'm going there next," Johnny Boy said. "Wanted to check on Linda first."

"I'll go, too," Mick said.

"The state police are there. They won't let you in the door."

"Then deputize me."

"I can't do that, Mick."

"You're the sheriff, Johnny Boy. You can deputize who you want. I'm the most experienced investigator in the county."

Mick watched him consider the idea, mentally picking it apart in a pragmatic fashion. A dozen reasons said no — the victim was a family member, Mick's relationship to the victim, his hill-bred instinct for vengeance. Still, Johnny Boy needed a deputy at short notice.

"Temporary acting deputy," he said.

"Thanks," Mick said. "I'll need a badge to get past the state troopers."

Johnny Boy removed his badge and handed it to Mick.

"Take this," he said. "I'll get Linda's. You'll need a weapon."

"I've got one."

"I know you play fast and loose, Mick. You can't do that if you're working on the county nickel."

Mick nodded.

"I mean it, Mick."

"I will keep you apprised of all information I acquire during the course of investigation, Sheriff Tolliver."

"I'll meet you there. Need to stop by the office and get Sandra started on the paperwork."

Johnny Boy stood, straightened his posture as befit the top lawman in the county, and went outside to his vehicle. Raymond shook his head and whistled through this teeth, a shrill sound in the muted acoustics of the waiting room.

"Fucking deputy," he said. "You been out what, two days? And already got a job."

"I could use a driver."

"All right. I'll ask J.C. to come wait here."

Raymond made the call as they left the hospital. Mick got in the truck, realizing it was the first time since he was a teenager that he'd ridden on the passenger side. He remembered using the glove box door as a shelf for a bottle of Ale-8 and a Hostess cupcake. When his grandfather accelerated, the pop and cake spilled on Mick's pants. Papaw laughed and laughed, then went back to the store and bought Mick another snack.

Mick opened the glove box and removed his army-issue sidearm, a Beretta M9. In a routine motion he ejected the clip, checked the barrel, rammed the clip back in place, and set the safety.

"Where to?" Raymond said.

"Take 60 out of town. Turn where the drive-in used to be. It's on the county line."

Raymond drove without talking. The late afternoon sun was visible above the western treeline, the hill throwing a deep shadow that spread across the land as if dousing flame. Raymond had never cared for small talk. Between his mother and Juan Carlos, he was seldom required to speak, just carry out instructions. He glanced at Mick's taut face, jaw clenched, an expression like a blast furnace in his eyes. Raymond hoped Linda came through — not for her sake or her brother's, but to protect the world from Mick's unleashed fury.

Nearly to Elliott County, he drove up the hill and along the ridge, leaving the darkened holler behind. The setting sun still illuminated the hilltop filled with official vehicles. A state trooper's lightbar flashed like neon lights in a dance club. Three EMTs leaned against an ambulance. Portable lights on stands lit two lines of crime scene tape that marked a bloody path across the yard ending at Linda's SUV. The door was open. A dark pool glistened under the interior dome light. His sister had crawled to her car to call dispatch.

Despite seeing gallons of blood in war, Mick couldn't recall the last time he'd seen family blood. A sense of anguished misery passed through him, swiftly replaced by anger. He preferred anger, something he could control. Mick let himself feel it, then set his emotions aside as if locking in a concrete bunker and went to the house.

A young city policeman tried to stop Mick, who showed his deputy badge and asked for Chet, knowing that using the chief's first name would carry weight.

"Inside," the cop said. He pointed at Raymond. "Who's he?"

"Special assistant," Mick said.

Blood smeared the porch steps and held the edge of a shoe print. Mick went to the side and climbed onto the porch, ducking under the wood rail. Raymond followed. Once inside, Mick flashed his badge to the state trooper in a dark gray uniform, the crease of the trousers sharp as tin. He didn't acknowledge Mick, a lowly deputy. Just inside the door was the beginning of the blood trail that led across the yard. Further into the room lay the body of a man. It was crumpled in the center of the front room, legs splayed across a rug. Blood pooled beneath him with rivulets running into cracks between the floorboards. Gravity had drawn the blood toward the center, which meant the floor was uneven. Probably dry rot in the joists.

Squatting beside the body was Marquis Sledge, the county coroner. He looked weary, having come here straight from Hack's place. Careful to stay back from Marquis's work, Mick bent from the waist, staring at the corpse, assembling in his mind a possible sequence of events. Various scenarios presented themselves, all with the same ending — the man died and Linda lived.

Mick straightened and faced Chet, who stood with Sergeant Faron Blevins in the entrance to the kitchen. Mick had met the sergeant a couple of years before, a solid enough cop though inexperienced with homicide. Murder was uncommon in Rocksalt and when it did occur, it was usually family or a neighbor and everyone knew who did it.

"Johnny Boy said you were coming," Chet said. "Faron here was first on scene."

"What've you got?" Mick said.

"Pretty much what you see," Faron said. "Linda was shot here. Crawled out to her car and called in."

"Who's on the floor?"

"Leo Gowan. It's his house. A gravel-truck driver, works out of Morgan County. I'd say he shot Linda. She returned fire and killed him."

"I'm going to look around a minute," Mick said. "Y'all know Raymond. He's with me."

"Is he a deputy, too?"

"Informal," Mick said. "Raymond, let me know when Marquis is done. I need to talk to him."

Mick went into the kitchen. The sink was empty. Clean dishes lay in a plastic rack, the silverware divided by utensil, knives stored blade down in the perforated drainer. Coffee pot. Sugar. Half a loaf of bread. The cabinets contained canned food along with cereal and crackers. He opened the refrigerator — milk, eggs, pop, cheese, baloney, and condiments. The freezer held ice cream, hamburger meat, and four popsicles. He

126

went down a short hall to a bedroom with a large unmade bed. The closet door was open. Men's work shirts on hangers along with one dress shirt and a single dark jacket and slacks — an all-purpose outfit for weddings and funerals. On the floor were two pairs of boots, ball shoes, and an old pair of lined moccasins. A twelve-gauge shotgun leaned in a corner. A narrow shelf held a box of shells, several work caps, and gloves — all well used.

Across the hall was a smaller room with a single bed, the covers pulled tight. The top blanket was designed to resemble a sports car with tires on the sides. Mick went back to the main bedroom and searched the dresser. Men's T-shirts, socks, and underwear. Two boxes of .45-caliber ammunition, one unopened, one three-quarters full. Raymond stuck his head in the door.

"Marquis's done," he said.

Mick hurried outside and caught up with Marquis by his car.

"You shouldn't be here," Marquis said.

"Johnny Boy deputized me."

"Doesn't matter. You're not clearheaded on this."

"What killed him?"

"A single gunshot wound to the chest. My guess is it hit both lungs, causing tension

127

pneumothorax."

"Sucking chest wound times two?"

"Just a guess. Can't confirm until examination."

"Did you find a gun under him?" Mick said. "A forty-five?"

"No gun," Marquis said.

"Anything from Hack Darvis?"

"Shotgun, close range."

"Same one that killed Pete Lowe?"

"No way to know," Marquis said. "I got to go. I'm beat. You need to get out of here before you get thrown out."

Mick turned back to the house, surprised to find Raymond standing two feet from him.

"You sneaking up on me?" Mick said.

"No way, dude. I'm making sure you don't do something crazy."

"I never done anything crazy in my damn life."

"Maybe you're due."

A pair of headlights rose along the ridge, topped the hill, and sliced across the yard. Mick and Raymond turned away, blinking. The car stopped and a door slammed. Johnny Boy came across the yard, slow and steady, a straight line over the grass.

"She's still in surgery," he said. "Anything here?"

"Marquis just finished," Mick said. "Gowan was killed by a pistol. No gun found but there's forty-five ammo inside. And a twelve-gauge shotgun."

"A shotgun killed Pete Lowe and Hack Darvis. Maybe all this is tied up together."

Mick nodded. Johnny Boy gestured to the state trooper's car, a dark gray Chevrolet Caprice.

"That trooper any help?" Johnny Boy said.

"I don't know. Ain't moved or spoke since I got here."

"Chet in there?"

"Yeah, him and Faron both."

They crossed the yard and entered the house. The EMTs had loaded the body onto a gurney and were discussing how to get it outside without disturbing the scene.

"Go out the back," Chet said.

"You're shitting me," the medical crew chief said. "Walk around in the dark? No telling what's laying there to trip over. That what you want? Us to spill the body in the damn yard?"

"You can't go through the front on account of evidence," Faron said. "If you don't like the back door, try going through a window."

Chet looked at the state trooper.

"How about putting your spotlight on the

129

side yard?" Chet said.

The trooper gave a slight nod, discernible only by the tipping of his wide-brimmed hat, then left without a word. Faron removed a long metal flashlight from a loop in his duty belt.

"I'll light the way for you," he said.

He and Chet went out the back door while the EMTs lifted the gurney and carried it down the hall. Twice it banged against the wall. Somebody cursed low. The door slammed shut and Mick could see them awkwardly crossing the side yard into the bright glare of the spotlight fastened to the trooper's car.

Mick returned to the front room and slowly turned in a circle, imagining what had happened. The room contained a couch, an easy chair, and a gigantic flatscreen television. There were three side tables. A narrow shelf unit held hunting magazines, a Bible, a framed school photo of a young boy, and a toy truck with a hand-painted name on it — Travis. Mick used his phone to photograph the position of the furniture and the bloody areas on the floor. He got on his hands and knees to peer under the couch, then asked Raymond to tip it back a few inches. He studied the imprint of the couch legs on the pine floor.

Footsteps clattered across the floor and Johnny Boy spoke.

"Good thing that trooper's setting in his car. He'd not like you messing with the crime scene."

"What's he doing here?" Mick said.

"Trying to be a big shot with Chet. He thinks he's hot shit but he ain't cold piss. What are you doing?"

"Looking for a gun," Mick said. "You find one?"

"No."

"Maybe Linda got it," Raymond said. "Lost it in the yard."

"We'll look at first light," Johnny Boy said.

"Something ain't right," Mick said. "It's off."

"What's off?" Johnny Boy said.

"Position of his body in the middle of the room. Her getting shot below the knee."

"She came in and shot him first. He fell and fired from the floor."

"Could be," Mick said. "I got to get back to the hospital."

Mick left, careful to avoid the congealing blood on the porch. He instinctively went to the driver's side of his truck, then walked to the passenger side. Raymond got in and began the long drive to town. Mick sat stiff as the doughboy statue on the old courthouse lawn.

"What'd you see back there?" Raymond said.

"Same thing you did."

"Not hardly, Mick. My job was to create havoc, then exfil. I never stuck around to see anything."

"She was shot in the leg at close range. That means a wild shot or deliberately aiming low, which is unlikely in a gunfight. Or hiding behind furniture. But that couch hadn't been moved till you did."

"How do you know?"

"Imprints of the feet on the floor."

"Maybe Gowan fired around the corner from the kitchen."

Mick nodded. They didn't talk during the rest of the drive to town. Sitting side by side in the hospital waiting room were Juan Carlos and Sandra, both asleep. Juan Carlos opened his eyes, blinked several times, and jostled Sandra.

"Out of surgery," she said. "They're moving her to a room soon. Prognosis is good."

"Will she walk?" Mick said.

"A lot of rehab but yes. She'll be okay, Mick."

A sense of relief staggered Mick, sweeping up from his boots and through his torso as if his body had turned to water. He stumbled, then sat heavily beside Sandra. He wanted to cry but knew he couldn't. He'd lost the ability in the desert. Suddenly exhausted he closed his eyes, intending to rest a minute then talk to a doctor. He was awakened by Sandra speaking his name.

"Mick," she said. "Mick, Mick, wake up."

He jolted to full alertness as if electricity coursed through him. He looked around, disoriented. He was in the hospital. Raymond and Juan Carlos were gone. Mick had the sense that time had passed but he was unsure if it was hours or minutes. He'd undergone a similar sensation after combat — the exhilarated fear fading, a sudden hard nap, then a greater vigilance.

"She's in her own room," Sandra said. "You can go in there."

"How long?"

"How long what?"

"Was I asleep?"

"I don't know. Couple of hours. Come on. You can rest in there. They got better chairs and it's quieter."

Mick followed Sandra to an elevator, upstairs, and through a maze of entwined corridors to a room with a heavy door. Linda lay in a bed with her eyes closed. Her left leg was heavily bandaged. She wore an oxygen mask. Tubes connected her arms to plastic bags hanging from silver hooks on two metal stands. A screen monitored her vital signs. Mick maneuvered a surprisingly plush and comfortable chair near the bed and took his sister's hand. Her skin was pale. She looked small in the tilted bed and he couldn't recall the last time he'd seen her asleep. Probably when they were kids.

CHAPTER ELEVEN

Johnny Boy had driven back to the crime scene in an adrenalized state that began to diminish during a prolonged search of the house until late in the night. The city police and the trooper had left. He was tired and wanted to rest but couldn't lie down in the dead man's home. He sat in his car for a catnap and awoke three hours later, his body stiff as hickory. For the first time in his life he felt old. He spent several minutes standing beside his car listening to the throbbing song of morning birds. With less than twenty-four hours on the job he was ready to quit being sheriff.

The sound of an engine filled the woods, hushing the birds momentarily. A city police car came into view and two men got out, Faron and a younger man named Dixon, the newest on the force. Dixon was over six feet tall and stout through the shoulders with the strongest arms in the county. During a charity event he'd lifted a two-hundred-pound generator and carried it farther than anyone else. The other participants — young athletes and firemen mainly — staggered slowly but Johnny Boy recalled seeing Dixon stroll as if carrying a bird nest.

Now he held a large cup of coffee with a lid and two sausage sandwiches from town. He offered them to Johnny Boy, who felt a surge of warmth he'd never known for another human, a sensation that made him anxious. He sipped the coffee, grateful that it had cooled in transit.

"Chet sent us," Faron said. "What do you need done?"

"I went through the house last night. What's left is an outside search."

"What are we looking for?"

"Anything. We don't know what happened or who all was here. There's .45 ammo inside and no gun. The gun is top priority. I need to go to town and find out Gowan's next of kin. There's some kid stuff in there. I'd say he's got an ex-wife and a boy somewhere."

Johnny Boy finished the sandwiches and gulped the coffee. The combination hit his guts and he hurried to the house. Dixon watched him go.

"Why'd he stay overnight?" Dixon said.

136

"Secure the scene," Faron said. "Folks find out Gowan's dead, they'll be up here looking to steal stuff. Remember that. You'll have to do it yourself one day."

Dixon stuck his bottom lip out and nodded in contemplation.

"Get you a long stick," Faron said. "Walk one side of the yellow tape then the other. Use the stick to push the weeds back. You need to cover every inch of this yard and into the woods."

"How far into the woods should I go?"

"Till lunch."

Dixon frowned. He'd meant in terms of distance but figured time was just as good. He didn't mind. He'd grown up in the woods and felt more comfortable there than town. He'd learned long ago his height and natural strength were a burden and a curse — scrappy little guys tried to start trouble with him and everyone assumed he wasn't that smart. He'd finished community college with high grades, aced the city police exam, but knew that the Rocksalt Police Department had recruited him due to his size. He'd rather work for the sheriff's department. This was the first chance he'd had to make an impression and if there was anything in the woods, he'd find it. He'd stay there long past lunch, too.

Johnny Boy went through the house one more time. Morning sun had risen far enough over the hills to pour in the eastern windows. The interior appeared larger with all the shadows dispersed but it was still small — four rooms in need of care. Molding had pulled away from wallboard, two kitchen cabinets hung open from latches that didn't quite catch. Both closets were missing door knobs.

He needed to check Gowan's shotgun against the pellets from the bodies of Pete Lowe and Hack Darvis. It was impossible to know if it was the same weapon, but he could at least match the gauge. He carried the gun outside, opened the trunk to stow the weapon, and saw the locked oak box containing the rattlesnake. He jumped back instinctively, banged his head on the trunk lid, and nearly dropped the shotgun.

"Shit," he yelled.

"Sir?" Dixon said from the woods.

"Nothing. You find anything?"

"All kinds of stuff. They dumped garbage in here for years."

"Go through it all," Johnny Boy said. "Make two piles. One for the past few months, then anything that looks real recent. Don't worry about anything rusted or rotted. Look for a forty-five and shotgun shell

138

casings."

"Yes, sir."

Johnny Boy couldn't recall when someone had called him "sir," if ever. He didn't mind it. He used his radio to call dispatch and told Sandra to ask Marquis what size pellets he'd found in Hack and Pete Lowe. She cut transmission and Johnny Boy wondered if she would ever call him "sir." Probably not. Still, it was the first time he'd given her instructions without some kind of back-and-forth guff. Maybe being sheriff wasn't so bad. Next he'd get the big fancy car.

He drove to his cousin's house. Caney Rodale was technically his second cousin once removed, a distinction made by Caney's mother. When her husband died she'd put part of his insurance into a new computer and devoted herself to amateur genealogy. Johnny Boy avoided her. She'd gotten snobby over her command of family connections, and taken to dispensing information in veiled criticisms. She'd once told Johnny Boy that he was just like his great-uncle's cousin — slow as smoke.

He left the blacktop for a gravel road that followed a creek up a holler. The third house in was Caney's. Leading to the porch were broad slabs of limestone that had shifted in the earth, creating a series of potential traps to twist an ankle and cause a fall. Beside the slabs was a path of beat-down grass. Johnny Boy walked it, climbed on the porch, and yelled through the screen door. Caney stepped outside eating a corn dog.

"Hey, Johnny Boy. It's Wednesday. That means corn dog day at the gas station. You wanting one? I know you like them. Still yet hot."

Johnny Boy almost said yes but worried that the corn dog might get in a fight with the sausage sandwiches. He was still recovering.

"Don't reckon," Johnny Boy said. "Them rocks in the yard are pretty tricky to walk on."

"Mom said to leave them like that. Said it was a way to know who's family and who ain't. If somebody walks on the rocks, I'm supposed to run them off. Is that your county car?"

"Yeah, but I'll be getting a new one soon." Johnny Boy leaned forward and tilted his torso to let the sun hit the sheriff's badge pinned on his shirt. To his disappointment, Caney ignored it.

"I'm getting a new car, too," Caney said. "One of them Ford Excruciators."

"A what?" Johnny Boy said.

"It's a big SUV with four-wheel drive."

"I don't think that's a real car. It's not even a real word."

"A lot of cars ain't real words. Like Camaro."

"You got a point. It was supposed to be Panther but they changed it so all the Chevy's would start with a *C*. You know, Corvette. Corsair."

"Panther's not a bad name."

"Uh, yeah, I guess so. How's your sister? I heard she had twins."

"She did, two boys. Good-looking babies. Kind of puny on account of two in there together. But they're growing fast. Mom's bent out of shape about it."

"I can see how twins might complicate her genealogy charts."

"It ain't that," Caney said. "She's worried over who they might get married to."

"Little early for that."

"Well, not for Mom. You know how she gets."

"Buddy, I do. What's wrong with twins getting married?"

"One wife can cheat with the brother. If she gets pregnant they can't prove nothing. The genealogies are the same."

"Never thought of that."

"My sister didn't either and she's tripping."

"Tripping? On acid?"

"No," Caney said. "It means upset. City people say it on TV."

"I'll keep that in mind."

"But you ain't here to talk about cars and Mom and TV. You won't eat a corn dog. So it must be you getting briggity over that badge."

"Didn't think you noticed. You're talking to the high sheriff of Eldridge County."

"Shit, you ain't been high a day in your life."

"Only dopes smoke dope. You still selling snakes?"

"Hell, yeah. I got six right now. You need one?"

Johnny Boy led Caney to the car and opened the trunk.

"You seen this before?"

"Naw, that's an old-timey snake box. I sell mine in burlap sacks."

"Can't they bite through that?"

"Yeah, I put the sack in a cardboard box from the liquor store. If it'll hold six quarts of whiskey, it'll hold a snake. You wanting to sell that box? Take it to a swap meet. People collect everything now. I seen old VHS tapes go for good money."

"Naw, it's got a snake inside. I want you to take a look at it."

142

"Just loose in there?"

"It's got screen on the inside."

"What size mesh?"

"I don't know, Caney. It looks pretty thick to me."

"Then why's it all tied up?"

Johnny Boy shrugged, unwilling to admit to his fear. Caney shook his head as if disgusted, picked up the box, carried it around the car, and placed it on the hood. He opened the case with no more care than a man flipping the lid off a can of Pringles. The snake coiled lazily and watched the human through the wire.

"Is it one of yours?" Johnny Boy said.

"Yeah, that's Bethany."

"How can you tell?"

"Looks, mainly. Same way you tell dogs apart. She's about three or four years old."

"It's got seven rattles. Don't that mean seven years old?"

"Naw. A snake grows a new rattle every time it sheds its skin. Young ones grow fast."

"Who'd you sell this snake to?"

"Hack Darvis."

"Why was he wanting a snake?"

"He didn't. He come around wanting some venom."

"You got that?"

"Naw, too much trouble. Hack wanted to

know how to get it."

"You tell him?"

"Sure did. They call it milking, but not like a cow. What you do is put a rag over the top of a jar. Then get the snake to bite through the rag. The venom drips down in the jar. But you got to do it three times. Rattlesnakes, they just got so much venom and don't like to waste it. The first couple of bites are warnings. If they don't get the job done, that third bite will flat pour the poison to you."

"After you milk the venom, how do you store it?"

"Got to be cold."

"Like a refrigerator?"

"Yeah, or the freezer for long-term. What's going on, Johnny Boy? You been scared to death of snakes since we were boys. Now you're driving around with one."

"Somebody killed Hack."

"Over Bethany?"

"I don't know. Can you keep this snake here? Don't sell it till I say it's okay."

Caney nodded and closed the box. Johnny Boy got behind the wheel.

"Say hidy to your sister and them babies," he said.

Johnny Boy drove back to town thinking that after two hours of investigating he didn't know anything except how to extract venom from a snake, a skill he'd never use. It did explain the refrigerator in Hack's shed. Maybe Hack was trying to make himself immune.

Johnny Boy didn't like to drive with less than half a tank of gasoline in case he got involved in a long chase. It had never happened in county history and he didn't want to be the first to run out of fuel. He stopped for gas at one of the few places that still had an unleaded pump for farm machinery. For sale inside was a variety of tools including such rarities as a T-post puller and a long-handled water-valve shut-off key. He bought a Dr Pepper and a bag of peanuts.

As he stepped outside he saw the blue Wagoneer again, the same one he'd seen in Fleming County a few nights back. It was the same driver, too. A long-haired, older man with a scraggly beard. He was waiting to turn onto the Main Road, glancing both ways, which gave Johnny Boy a good look at him in the bright sun. He didn't know the man but he knew the features. The name Rodale floated through his mind but he dismissed it since he'd just seen his cousin Caney Rodale. If he had a photo, he could ask Caney to show it to his mother. The Wagoneer drove onto the blacktop and

Johnny Boy noticed that the car lacked a license plate. It was enough to pull him over. Johnny Boy considered the idea, but decided he had too much to do — three homicides, a shot sheriff, and a long trip across the county.

At the Reeder place he parked in the same place as before, his old tracks still visible in the soft dirt. Mr. Reeder was standing on a chair with his upper body bent beneath the open hood of the Bronco. He appeared to be wearing the same clothes as yesterday.

"Mr. Reeder," he called.

The man didn't move. Johnny Boy coughed loud and scuffed his feet.

"Reach me a crescent wrench," Mr. Reeder said.

Johnny Boy dug through the open toolbox and found two of different sizes.

"Which one?" he said.

Mr. Reeder lifted his head from the engine.

"Big one," he said. "I thought you were Roscoe."

"Is he here?"

"In the house," Mr. Reeder said. "You can go on in. My opinion he's plugged into those damn thimbles."

Johnny Boy gave him the wrench, went to the screen door, and yelled through the mesh. There was no answer and he peered in. Propped on the couch with multiple pillows lay Roscoe wearing earbuds and staring at his phone. A coffee table held a plate with a few crumbs and a fork. Johnny Boy entered and kicked the couch.

"Quit it, Daddy," Roscoe yelled, staying focused on his phone.

Johnny Boy pulled one earbud free.

"I'm the sheriff, not your daddy."

"Thought you were the deputy."

"I was. The sheriff got shot. I need to talk to you."

"I didn't do it. I ain't left the house. Ask Daddy."

"Not about that," Johnny Boy said. "About rooster fighting."

"I ain't no expert."

"Who is?"

"Hack Darvis, I reckon."

"Hack's dead."

"Hack and Pete both?"

"That's right. Did you kill them?"

"Hell, no! Why would I?"

"Why would anybody?"

Roscoe swung his legs to the floor and stared at Johnny Boy, who tapped his badge with a forefinger.

"You'd best talk to me," Johnny Boy said.

"Why? I ain't done nothing."

"Possession of a dead man's bird to start. Resisting arrest if you say one more word I don't like."

"Damn," Roscoe said. "You don't have to sheriff me so hard. Where's that other feller at?"

"At the hospital with his sister. Who killed Hack? Who killed Pete?"

"I don't know any of that."

"Why did Hack have a rattlesnake?"

"Some fellers said he smeared snake poison on the gaffs."

"What's that?"

"They strap them to a rooster's legs. Sharp as razors. Cut a rooster with poison on the gaff and it dies real quick. They said Hack done that."

"Wouldn't a rooster poison itself by accident?"

"Naw, chickens are a whole lot smarter than people think."

Johnny Boy grunted as if in vague assent. Roscoe had inadvertently ruled himself out of suspicion. Anyone who believed in the intelligence of chickens wasn't smart enough to sneak up on an armed man.

"Did Pete know about the poison?"

"Yeah, Pete said no way Hack would kill birds. He was making too much money off the fights."

"From betting?"

"No, that's all between the men. Hack gets half the entry fee. Sells cigarettes, beer, and whiskey. Charges an arm and a leg, too."

"When's the next fight?"

"I don't know."

"You said it was online."

"Not anymore. That whole chat room is gone."

"When did that happen?"

"After Pete got killed."

Johnny Boy pulled an official business card from his shirt pocket and gave it to Roscoe.

"You hear about another fight," Johnny Boy said, "you call me."

"This says you're a deputy, not the sheriff."

"I ain't had time to get new cards yet."

Johnny Boy left the house. Mr. Reeder stood on a wooden chair, one leg in the air for balance, his entire torso inside the engine compartment. The chair shifted and Johnny Boy moved quickly to hold it.

"You all right in there, Mr. Reeder?" he said.

"Yeah."

"This chair ain't stable."

"I know it. But the stepladder's either too

high, too short, or sets sideways."

"I got to go in a minute. Want me to get Roscoe?"

"Naw, he ain't worth the powder it'd take to shoot him. Here."

Mr. Reeder's greasy hand held two nuts and two washers. Johnny Boy obediently dropped them in an empty tinfoil pan. Four locknuts lay beside two broken bolts that were shiny where they'd snapped from pressure. On the ground was an electric drill attached to a long extension cord that disappeared in the high grass by the house.

"Can I talk to you, Mr. Reeder?"

"Son, that's all you been doing."

"I mean more face-to-face like."

With a grunt and prolonged sigh, Mr. Reeder rose from inside the engine, his face marred by streaks of black. He held a hammer with a handle wrapped in electrician's tape and a pair of vise grips.

"Don't need y'all's help," he said. "Roscoe ain't evicted no more. I didn't know Misty was gone. He was ashamed to tell me."

"That's not why I'm here."

Mr. Reeder sat on the radiator and stared unblinking. He was the kind of man who'd wait a week to speak about anything other than giving instructions. Johnny Boy's father had been the same way, some kind of

150

generational throwback, a trait that had bypassed Johnny Boy. He was suddenly irritated, the same way he got with his dad.

"Another man's dead," Johnny Boy said. "Hack Darvis. You know him?"

"Naw, I stayed away from Hack. They say he cut a tree that fell on a man on purpose."

"You believe that?"

"What I believe don't matter. What I know is this — two fellers went in the woods and only one come out alive."

"He ain't no more," Johnny Boy said. "Hack's dead."

"You think my boy's mixed up in that?"

"He's in with bird fighting. Roscoe might know who killed Hack and not know he knows it."

"That's true for everybody, ain't it? You and me, too."

"Yeah," Johnny Boy said, "but we're not the ones keeping two roosters."

"Let me ask you something. I ain't trying to get nobody in trouble but cockfighting, it's illegal, right?"

"Yep."

"Why don't y'all do nothing about it?"

"It's a felony in forty-two states. But in Kentucky it's a misdemeanor. People come from all over to fight their birds here. If they get busted, a misdemeanor's not that bad.

You want to keep your son safe, tell him to get out of bird fighting. I got to go."

Johnny Boy lowered his chin in farewell and climbed the hill to his truck. Two sets of tire treads were visible in the dirt road. He pulled out his phone and photographed the tracks, then scrolled back to the photos he'd taken behind Hack Darvis's place. The tire tracks didn't match, which relieved him. It didn't exclude the Reeders completely but he didn't think they were involved. The next few photos were of the footprints, size seven. He went back down the hill and asked Roscoe what size Misty wore.

"I don't know," he said. "Her feet are little. She complained about it a lot."

"About her feet?"

"No, the shoes. Stores only bought one or two pair of small ones, then put them in the window. She said because they're cute and don't take up much room. They got sun-faded and she didn't like that. Sometimes she shopped in the kids' section."

"Did she leave any shoes behind when she left?"

"There's a box of her stuff."

Johnny Boy followed him to the chicken house. Roscoe pointed to a cardboard carton and began talking to the roosters. Johnny Boy found cut-off shorts, a skinny

152

belt with a butterfly buckle, two tabloid magazines, and a pair of worn sandals. He carried them outside for the light. They were tiny things, size five–six. He thanked Roscoe and left.

Chapter Twelve

Mick slept beside his sister's bed, waking
every hour when various medical personnel
entered the room. He tuned out the high-
pitched steady beep of the machinery and
focused on the generalized hum that perme-
ated all hospitals.

Morning brought sunlight and a new shift
of nurses into the room, some freshly caffeinated and chipper. He ignored them and
watched his sister's breathing. Her wounded
leg was wrapped and swaddled from upper
thigh to foot. Her toes were visible, which
he knew she wouldn't like. As a child she'd
been embarrassed by her feet — the big toe
was noticeably separate from the rest at a
slight angle like a thumb. She never wore
sandals or flip-flops. He suddenly recalled
an Australian mercenary who referred to his
flip-flops as thongs, much to the consterna-
tion of his American comrades.

Mick stood and stretched to clear his

mind of drifty thinking. He peered through the window at the parking lot. The golden light of dawn merged with the garish yellow emanating from encased bulbs on steel poles. A sensor triggered and all the lights doused themselves, leaving softer shadows and prettier air. He watched people walk to their cars, their pace slow after twelve hours on their feet.

Behind him the bedsheets rustled. He turned to see Linda shifting her arm as if trying to release herself from the confines of the bed.

"Stay still," he said. "You're in the hospital."

"What?" she mumbled. "Where . . ."

Her voice trailed away. He waited long enough to ensure she was asleep before summoning a nurse. During the next two hours he sat close, his eyes never leaving his sister. There was no past. There was no future. He occupied the present beside his wounded sister the same way he had while waiting for combat.

A few hours later, Linda stirred, then slowly came awake, blinking several times as awareness filtered into her vision.

"You're all right, Sis," Mick said. "You're in the hospital. You got shot."

"Where?"

"Left leg. They did surgery. You're under sedation."

"How bad?"

"Not good. But you'll walk."

She nodded and appeared to rest briefly, then snapped her eyes open and Mick understood that she was feeling pain, that the drugs were wearing off. In its own way, it was a good sign.

"What happened?" he said.

"Went in the house."

"Who was there?"

She shook her head and closed her eyes. He left the room and called the sheriff's office. Sandra answered.

"She woke up and talked," Mick said. "Groggy but okay."

"Good to hear. I'll come by after my shift."

"Thanks. Did Johnny Boy find anything at the scene?"

"The city police brought in four bags of junk from the woods. Johnny Boy's out looking into Pete Lowe and Hack Darvis. Said you were investigating Linda's shooting. Isn't that a conflict of interest?"

"Technically, yes. I need whatever you can dig up on Leo Gowan."

"Got it right here," she said.

"Be there later."

Mick ended the call. Anxiety rippled along

his limbs as he realized there was no one to relieve him at the hospital. He called Raymond and explained the situation.

"I can't leave," Raymond said. "J.C.'s got me prepping for lunch. We can get there after four o'clock."

"What about your mom?"

There was a silence while Raymond considered the idea. Mick could hear conjunto music over the phone and Juan Carlos occasionally singing along. Down the hall, two nurses stood with their mobile carts and laughed, the sound odd in the air. It was a good reminder — people laughed at work regardless of the job. Mick recalled grim humor from fellow investigators while facing grisly crime scenes.

"I'll ask," Raymond said. "But Mommy won't like it."

"Nobody likes hospitals."

"She doesn't like cops, either."

"Then tell her it's a hurt woman who ain't got nobody else. She owes me one, remember."

"She really won't like that. But I'll call her."

Mick returned to the room. A young man in casual clothes identified himself as Dr. Lannan, a hospitalist. He held a sheaf of papers on an incongruously old clipboard.

157

Linda's prognosis was good, with no post-surgery complications. Her pain management medicine was switched to Percocet. A blood transfusion had saved her life.

"What's next?" Mick said.

"Rest. Then rehab."

"How long?"

"Weeks, maybe months. You'll need to talk to the surgeon."

"When?"

"He'll make his rounds later this afternoon. I know you're worried. But she's in good shape. Strong and healthy. Extensive debriding of tissue was necessary. But it looks like she can make a full recovery."

Dr. Lannan turned away and Mick watched the small man walk slowly from the room, flipping pages on the clipboard, preparing for his next patient. Linda changed position, the pain making her body seek comfort, her brain not yet knowing that none was available. He sat and waited for Raymond's mother, Shifty Kissick. Mick's father had courted her forty years before but she'd chosen a more stable man who died young. Mick had done her a small favor a few years back, then a bigger one later, which entailed protecting her from a criminal's retribution. With Raymond out of the Marines and back home, she was more safeguarded, not that she needed it. Every time Mick saw her she'd been armed.

An orderly came and went, drifting through the room, bearing fresh towels and emptying the trash can. Light through the window touched the corner of the bed and Mick adjusted the curtains. In repose, his sister's face lost age as if rescinding adulthood and returning to the status of a child. An errant strand of hair wisped over her face. He resisted the urge to move it aside, preferring to avoid any disturbance.

Shifty Kissick entered the room without knocking. She wore a long straight dress and a pair of dress shoes suitable for town. Over the dress was a light blue sweater with the corner of a handkerchief protruding from the cuff

"Thank you for coming, Mrs. Kissick."

She set a large purse on the foot of the bed, leaned over Linda, and with a delicate touch moved the stray hair from her face.

"Just to get things straight," she said, "I'm here for her, not you."

"That's generous of you."

"Who did it? A man, I bet."

Mick nodded.

"Well, son, you best get out there and find the son of a bitch."

"Yes, ma'am. I'll tell the nurse you're family. That way they can't make you leave."

"Done did," she said. "I'm your Aunt Shifty. Now, get."

Mick left, thinking about the contents of her bag. He'd been raised never to touch a woman's pocketbook. His grandfather said it was best not to even look at it. Mick was twelve and asked why. "It's untelling what's in there," Papaw had said. "My granny kept an icepick stuck in a cork." Mick had nodded, following the primary habit of the men in his family, and memorized the rare piece of information about females. Now, as he left the hospital, he figured Shifty's purse contained a small pistol with the sights filed off so it wouldn't snag.

Mick drove to the sheriff's office, where Sandra sat at her desk looking at a computer screen and using a pen to scribble notes on a pad. One shoulder was lifted to accommodate a landline telephone receiver pressed to her ear. Her cell phone buzzed from an incoming call. In a sudden smooth series of motions she ended all her activities and read aloud from the pad.

"Leo Gowan. Thirty-one years old. Employed by J. B. Paving in West Liberty. Divorced two years ago. One child, Travis, age eight. Ex-wife, Carla Jo, age twenty-seven, remarried to Lester Wallace. They live in Clearfield. One thing of interest. Carla Jo had a restraining order against Leo."

"Good work, Sandra."

They stared at each other silently, uncertain how to proceed, their brief history a barrier compounded by circumstances. With professional interaction over, Mick didn't know what to say. He waited.

"How's Linda?" Sandra said. "Did you talk to the doctor?"

"She's in for a hard row to hoe."

"Who shot her?"

"She's still drugged up. She'll remember more in a couple of days. Did Johnny Boy do a next of kin for Gowan?"

"No, they live in Morgan County. State police did it. Johnny Boy's chasing down Hack and Pete's killer. Or killers."

"Does he think there's two now?"

"He didn't say but you never know. What do you think, Mick?"

"Both victims were involved with cockfighting. Both male and lived alone. Cause of death was the same. My gut says one man killed both."

"Your gut ever been wrong?"

He nodded.

"One other thing," she said. "Johnny Boy says he knows more about the rattlesnake.

Said you'd understand."

He nodded again, ready to leave, but feeling as if he should be extra polite to Sandra.

"Well," he said. "See ya."

He turned to leave.

"What should I tell Johnny Boy?" she said.

"About what?"

"You. He's the sheriff and you're his deputy. I'm dispatch. He'll want to know what you're up to."

"I'm going to talk to Leo's ex-wife."

Sandra's desk phone rang. She answered it and Mick walked outside to his truck. It had been years since he'd reported his movements to a superior. A few days ago, he'd have ignored Sandra's question, which wouldn't have been asked in the first place by a lower rank. Civilian life, he reminded himself. It was more fluid, less defined, the communication channels vague and informal. He already didn't like it.

CHAPTER THIRTEEN

Mick drove 519, a major blacktop strip through the hills known locally as the Old Clearfield Road. Younger residents called it the West Liberty Road. A select group referred to it as the Pink Palace Highway, named for the exterior walls of a prison built twenty-five years ago. He reached the turn-off for Morgan Fork and realized he'd gone too far, unfamiliar with the new construction. He backtracked to Dry Creek Road and followed it to an unpaved road, at the end which lived Leo Gowan's ex-wife, Carla Jo.

The one-story house had a pitched roof that extended over a porch running the length of the front. Part of the yard was fenced to enclose a swing set, a wading pool, and a small bicycle. A toy sword and a coonskin hat lay on the grass. There was a dog's water bowl but no dog in sight. Mick left his truck. The porch steps were sturdy, made of treated lumber that had been heavily shellacked.

He stomped the porch twice then knocked lightly on the screen door. From within came the warning bark of a dog. Mick stepped back. A woman opened the door and a small dog shot through the narrow space. It ran to the end of the porch, spun in the air, and resumed barking with shrill ferocity. It had a Chihuahua head mounted on the body of a blue heeler, like kids had assembled it from scraps. They began coloring with a black marker, got bored, and started daubing at his body, then quit altogether.

"Don't mind him," the woman said. "He won't bite."

"What kind is he?"

"A mutt. We got Cowboy at the kill shelter down the road."

"Pretty brave from seven or eight feet away."

"Part herd dog, and my boy's his whole herd."

"Not you, too?"

"I can't speak for Cowboy," she said, "but I think he sees me like the shepherd. Good for food and shelter and not much else."

With the pleasantries out of the way she regarded him carefully. She was in her early thirties, dressed in jeans and a sleeveless shirt. No tattoos, arm muscles defined in the way of a mother doing perpetual household labor. She stood with her weight evenly distributed, not hiding behind the door, staring at him straight on. He wondered if she had the wherewithal to kill a man. Everybody did.

"I'm Mick Hardin, deputy with the county. Are you Carla Jo Wallace?"

"Yes. You here about Leo?"

"Yes ma'am. I'm sorry."

"It's tougher on Travis than me."

"Leo was his father?"

Carla Jo pulled the front door shut, then gestured to three chairs on the porch.

"Travis is asleep right now. I don't want to wake him. And I don't want him hearing any talk about his dad."

She took the middle chair.

"Which one's your husband's?" Mick said.

She pointed and he sat in the other one. She nodded at his courtesy, face softening momentarily.

"Pretty place," he said. "Y'all must set out here a lot."

"Every evening after Lester gets home from work."

Three robins flew as if in private formation to the limbs of a crabapple tree. The

165

flowers were gone and the fruit hadn't quite arrived. The birds departed.

"Those robins are checking for food," Mick said.

"Sure are. I'll hang me some aluminum in the tree when the apples get full green. Scare the birds off."

"You gather them apples?"

"For jelly," she said. "Travis wants to build a tree house in it. My husband nailed a board up there. Told him when the tree grew he'd add more."

Mick nodded. It was a good solution, better than explaining to a child that he'd grow but a crabapple tree wouldn't.

"Ma'am," he said. "I need to ask a few things about Leo."

"Just call me Carla Jo."

"Y'all were married for five years?"

"Four and a half. Travis was born the first year."

"Where did you live?"

"A trailer on Brushy. After the divorce, he rented that other place."

"You ever visit there?"

"No," she said in a harsh tone.

"But Travis did."

"My husband dropped him off twice a month for four hours. He waited in the car for Travis."

"Because of the restraining order?"

"Leo wanted more time with Travis but the courts said no. Supervised visits only. Lester, he didn't have to wait in the car. He could have gone in but he was trying to be nice about it."

"Sounds like a good man."

"He is. Good to me, real good with Travis. Takes good care of this place, too."

"I can see that."

Mick watched the treeline, letting the silence drape over them. She was more comfortable now. He was relying on that for the next part of the conversation. The dog hopped onto Carla Jo's lap and settled with its tiny head aimed at Mick, still guarding her. A mourning dove moaned. The dog cocked one ear to the sound then ignored it.

"We need to talk about Leo a minute," Mick said. "I know it ain't an easy time. But I have to."

She nodded, tightening her lips.

"Can you think of anybody who might've wanted to hurt Leo?"

"I haven't seen or talked to him in three years."

"Lester has. Where was he two nights ago?"

"He comes home every evening after his shift."

"What do y'all do?"

"Same as ever. He plays with Travis. I make supper then we eat."

"And after supper?"

"Work in the yard if it's still pretty out. Watch TV. Put Travis to bed. Then set and talk."

"What do y'all usually talk about?"

"Bills. His job. Lately we've been planning on putting in a driveway and building a garage."

"What kind of guns does your husband own?"

"Deer rifle."

"What about a pistol?"

"No. Why are you asking me all this? You think Lester killed Leo?"

"No, ma'am. I don't. But somebody did. My sister got shot, too."

"I heard it was the sheriff. She's your sister?"

Mick nodded.

"I'm sorry," Carla Jo said. "She all right?"

"She'll make it. But you can understand why I got to bear down on this. Did Leo own a pistol?"

"Yeah. A big one. Family size, he called it."

"Big how?"

"He said it was a forty-five."

"Do you know where he kept it?"

"Truck mostly. At night in a drawer by the bed."

"At your all's trailer?"

She nodded.

"What about his new place?"

"I don't know. I was never in it. Have you talked to Penny?"

"Who's that?"

"Penny Lawson. His girlfriend."

Sensing Carla Jo's discomfort, the little dog licked her hand, its pink tongue the size of a cat's. Mick had never owned a pet. His grandfather had an old bluetick hound that liked to lie around in the shade. It never entered the house. Abruptly Mick wanted a dog — and even more preposterously — a small lapdog that would lick his hand in an obsessive manner.

"I need to talk to Penny," he said. "You know where she might be staying?"

"No, I never met her. Travis talked about her is all. Penny had a girl about his age. They played some. He liked her. You know, kids that age don't care about being a boy or a girl."

"What about your husband? Did he meet Penny?"

"I don't know. He'll be home at six thirty this evening."

"Could you do me a favor and call him? Maybe he knows where Penny lives."

"He can't always answer at work. Unless it's an emergency."

"He might not want the law coming in and talking to him. Most folks don't."

She considered his words then withdrew a cell phone from her back pocket. Mick stood, alarming the dog, and walked into the yard. A long rope hung from the lowest bough of the crabapple tree. On the ground below was a crooked ladder with three rungs. As a kid, Mick had climbed hundreds of trees. His favorite activity was finding two trees a few feet apart — a tall one and a young short one. He climbed the tall tree then leaped to the shorter one, grabbing the bole in both hands, his momentum causing the younger tree to bend toward the earth. If he chose correctly, the tree bowed from his weight and eased him down. Sometimes the young tree broke and he fell. Other times, it didn't bend far enough and he was stuck ten or fifteen feet above the earth and had to let go. It was the uncertainty that he liked — the leap into space, relying on his agility to grasp the tree, not knowing what would happen next. He'd lived that way most of his life.

Carla Jo called to him and he went to the edge of the porch.

"Penny's got an aunt who lives in Sharkey," Carla Jo said. "Lily, he thinks her name is. Atkins or Adkins, one. Maybe Atkinson."

"Thank you."

Mick got in his truck and called Sandra as he drove back toward town. He told her about Shifty staying at the hospital and asked for information about Lily Adkins or Atkins. He got on Flemingsburg Road, crossed under the interstate, and stopped for fuel at one of those new places that were replacing gas stations throughout the country. Off to the side was a machine with a long, thin hose to inflate your tires for $1.50 in quarters. To get change you went inside, where containers of water cost three bucks. Paying for water and air, Mick thought. No wonder people were mad in general.

Sandra called back with an address for Lily Atkins. He drove onto Sharkey Road, a two-lane blacktop with a network of tarred repairs. He passed a sign that said God was watching him, and briefly pondered the mass surveillance system being implemented throughout the country. Law enforcement in England had demonstrated its efficacy, despite the outcry from privacy advocates. Mick supposed it was a matter of time until the security tapes were altered to implicate an innocent person. He turned onto a smaller road and found the address.

Lily Atkins lived in one of the older houses, surrounded by prefab homes, a concept that eluded Mick. He figured it was in the gray area between a trailer and a house, the low-end equivalent to an urban duplex — neither house nor condo. The driveway was limestone gravel.

He parked and left the truck, weary of his usual caution. If there were dogs, he'd scare them off. Inside, a TV blared so loud that if the curtains had been open he could have watched the daytime shows. Nobody answered the door. He knocked louder, then used a nickel to rap on the glass. The volume of the TV lowered and he knocked again. A woman in her fifties opened the door with a broad, welcoming smile. She had short gray hair cropped in a slanting style that he'd only seen on young people.

"Hi," she said, "do I know you?"

"I'm Jimmy Hardin's boy, Mick."

"Oh, gosh. One of the Hardins from the other side of the county?"

"Yes, ma'am. Are you Lily Atkins?"

"Sure am."

"Do you like my hair? I just got it done. Ashley Fly is the best beauty operator around. She's a stylist!"

"Yes, ma'am. It's very nice. Popular, I think."

"I like a man who notices a woman's hair. So many don't these days. Come in, come in."

"Thank you, but I'm all right here for now. I'm trying to find your niece."

"I got seven. Which one?"

"Penny Lawson. I understand she lives here."

"Well . . ."

Her voice trailed away and her entire body seemed to shift as if presenting an invisible wall.

"Mrs. Atkins, I'm with the county. Your niece knows a man who died here lately."

"Got hisself killed, you mean. I heard."

"That's right. I want to ask Penny if he had trouble with somebody at work, maybe a neighbor."

"How'd you know she lived with me?"

"His ex-wife told me," Mick said.

"Carla Jo?"

"Has he got more than one?"

"No, just her. I know her mom from church. She said Carla Jo got married to Lester Wallace."

"Yes, ma'am, I believe she did. Is Penny home?"

"No, she's not."

"Do you remember when you saw her last?"

"Of course I do," she said. "There's nothing wrong with my memory."

"I apologize. I didn't mean it that way."

From inside the house came the clucking of a chicken louder than the television. Mick tilted his head to hear better. The sound continued, rising as if enthusiastic, then subsiding to a few satisfied gurgles.

"That's Riley," Mrs. Atkins said. "I thought he was a boy but she's a hen."

"You keep her inside?"

"Not all the time. Just when it's too hot for her. Everybody around here used to keep chickens. Now there's less of both, people and birds. Riley's the last chicken in Sharkey. She's important."

"An important chicken."

"Oh, yes! A long time back people here wanted a post office to get mail regular. They had to ask the government, a big rigamarole that went on for nigh six months. The government finally said yes but they needed a town name. We didn't have one. It was just roads and farms out here. One bunch with the biggest family wanted their

174

name used but people didn't like them. Everybody argued for a week. That Saturday was a rooster fight between Shanghai and Sharkey. The people decided to name the town after the winner."

"Sharkey won?"

"Yep. Killed Shanghai dead. My grand-mother told me. Her mother was there. So you see, Riley is keeping the spirit of Shar-key alive. The post office is gone now. We're back to being roads and farms."

Mick nodded, thinking of a chicken that Shifty Kissick had taught to walk backward. For three years he'd been meaning to ask her how she'd trained it. A dragonfly flitted by, its iridescent body flashing in the sun.

"Mrs. Atkins," Mick said. "I really need to talk to Penny."

"She left a few days ago. Her ex came and got some of her stuff. She called and said to let him take it. My opinion, they're getting back together. I hope so. That little girl needs her father."

"Yes, ma'am," Mick said. "Where does he live?"

"Randy? Down past Farmers on a little old road by the river."

"Randy. I must know six guys with that name."

"He's a Caldwell. The holler bunch, not

them ridge Caldwells."

"Thank you, Mrs. Atkins. You've been a big help."

She took a half step closer, cocked her head, and smiled.

"You must be married," she said. "A man like you."

"I'm divorced."

"You come back when you've got more time."

She gestured to her silver hair.

"There might be snow on the mountain top but there's still fire down below."

Mick drove to the first wide spot and pulled over beneath a shagbark hickory, one of his favorite trees. If the situation wasn't so dire, the interaction with Mrs. Atkins would be amusing. The next man who knocked at her door was in for a treat or trouble. Or maybe an egg. Mick had always wanted to be the kind of man who could drop everything and engage a woman physically. The problem was that he needed to know her first, needed to feel something ahead of time — like with Sandra. But he'd pretty much ruined that, along with his marriage and a brief affair with a British intelligence officer several months back. He thought she was MI6 because she carried four cell phones. The number she gave him didn't work for any of them.

He called Sandra and requested an address and directions to Randy Caldwell's place in Farmers. With the phone on speaker, he wondered if the man's full name was Randall, making him Randall Caldwell. He'd known a number of people whose first and last names rhymed, an odd tradition of the hills. Clinton Morton. Amy Ramey in Carter County, and a Sam Hamm from grade school. He recalled a boy named Abbot Abbot, as if his folks had run out of steam and gone with the simplest solution. Everyone called him Rabbit.

Sandra's voice came through the tinny speaker.

"There's two Randy Caldwells," she said. "One age fifty-nine, one thirty-four. Different houses, same road. Father and son."

"I need both addresses."

"You're a deputy now," she said. "What you need is an onboard coms unit with a GPS. You can access all the same records I can. Save you time and me work."

"Good idea."

"Or maybe you just like talking to me."

"Uh, what's the address?"

She gave it to him, along with a set of directions, then put him on hold. He was grateful for the respite from the discomfort of phone-flirting. After a minute she returned.

"That was Ray-Ray," she said. "His mom called him. Said Linda is awake and eating. That's a good sign, Mick."

"Thanks."

"Anything else?" she said.

"Did Johnny Boy go through the trash the city police brought in?"

"He's still yet in the field. There's five big garbage bags in his office."

"You said four before."

"Dixon brought in another one. Are you double-checking my math?"

"No," Mick said. "I'm hoping for a forty-five-caliber revolver."

"I'm not digging through it."

"Call Dixon and ask if he found one. In the house or out."

"All right," she said. "Is that it?"

He nodded and ended the call. Farmers was a straight shot south on 801 and a few minutes later it occurred to him that he'd forgotten to say goodbye to Sandra. One more mark in the negative column for him. It didn't matter. He was going to Corsica in two days.

At one time Farmers was the only place in the county where Ale-8 was available, and a few years later the only place to get a passport photo. Now it had gas stations, bait and tackle shops, and a renowned barbeque place called Pop's — all due to tourism centered around Cave Run Lake. Until the dam was built, the community of Farmers flooded every few years. Residents kept boats handy as a precaution. Many homes were washed away but a few of the older houses still remained, the high-water marks repainted, siding replaced, and yards resodded. Mick passed the home place of the older Caldwell, set far enough back from the river to have survived the earlier floods. A big pickup with a grill guard was parked in front. A mile down the road was a newer house with vinyl siding, vinyl-clad windows, and no porch. Mick wondered if it was a response to potential flood — the entire structure looked as if it could float safely downriver.

He parked on the shoulder and crossed the yard. A metal wheelbarrow lay upside down in the grass. Mick knocked three times, waited, and did it again — the universal sign of serious business — not a neighbor, politician, or fresh-faced Mormon boys. He listened, heard nothing, and knocked again. He sensed someone to the side and turned. A man stood at the corner of the house holding a shotgun aimed at

Mick. It was braced loosely over his left forearm, at the end of which he held a pistol.

Mick slowly spread his arms to show his empty hands.

"Hey," he said. "That's the first time somebody got the drop on me in a long time. Reckon I'm a little tired."

"What do you want?"

"Looking for Randy Caldwell. That you?"

"Who the fuck are you?"

"I'm Mick Hardin, county deputy."

"Bullshit," Randy said. "That old truck ain't official and I don't see no uniform or badge."

"I'm new on the job."

Mick waited. Randy's style of holding weapons meant he'd had no training and would hesitate to shoot, a delay long enough for Mick to dive into the grass, roll, and come to a kneeling position with his Beretta. He might receive the outer edge of the shotgun's expanding cone of pellets on his extremities. Or he might not. Either way, Randy was in trouble and didn't know it.

"What do you want?" Randy said.

"I'm trying to find your ex-wife. Her aunt Lily said you came by and got a bunch of Penny's things."

"She didn't kill that man."

"I don't think so either, but she might

180

know who did."

"Way that prick done Penny, he deserved it."

"Did you kill him?" Mick said.

"No, man. I wouldn't kill nobody."

"Then how about aiming that shotgun somewhere else?"

Randy glanced at the shotgun as if he'd forgotten about it, then lowered the barrel. Mick reached in his pocket for the badge Johnny Boy had given him at the hospital. He moved closer and displayed it.

"Johnny Boy Tolliver's the sheriff now," Mick said.

"God almighty. Johnny Boy? I'd say the county's in for a crime wave. What happened to that lady sheriff?"

"She got shot. She's my sister."

"Sorry, man."

"That's why I'm looking for Penny."

"She ain't here."

"Do you know where she is?"

Randy clicked his tongue against his cheek and looked away. He shook his head vigorously.

"No," he said.

Mick knew he was lying and took another step.

"Are you sure about that?" he said. "You pulled two guns on me."

"I didn't know who you were. Might be some Gowan coming around to finish things off."

"That means Penny was here. Where'd she go?"

"I don't know."

"Yeah, you do. She's somewhere with your little girl. You either tell me where or I'm taking you in."

"For what? This is my damn property."

In a sudden movement Mick yanked the shotgun from Randy's right hand and used the barrel to hit his left wrist. The pistol fell to the earth with enough impact to fire a bullet that struck the upturned wheelbarrow. Mick picked up the pistol, a .38 revolver.

"If you keep one in the chamber," he said, "don't drop the gun."

Randy held his wrist and moaned as Mick unloaded the pistol. He checked the shotgun's breach, unloaded the shells, then put both guns on the ground. He withdrew his Beretta and fired it into the air, startling Randy. Mick pointed the barrel at his leg.

"One in the leg and you're in the hospital with my sister. If you move, it might hit your knee and you'll never walk right again. I'm a pretty good shot so you need to hold stiller than you ever thought you could. Hear me?"

Randy nodded.

"Now where's Penny at?"

"She ain't here."

Mick fired into the ground beside Randy's boot.

"Not what I asked," Mick said.

The high-pitched whine of an engine under extreme acceleration sounded along the road. A pickup truck came into view — the one with a grill guard he'd seen earlier. It turned abruptly, left the blacktop, and roared across the yard. The driver braked and cut the wheel. The truck slid sideways and stopped. From the window the driver leveled a Winchester .30-30 rifle at Mick. He was an older man wearing a feed-store cap that kept his long gray hair tucked back.

"Put your damn gun down," the man said.

Mick dropped the Beretta and shifted his weight to present a smaller target — his left side and shoulder.

"You hurt, son?" the man said.

"I'm all right, Daddy," Randy said.

"Who's shooting at who?" the man said.

"Your boy shot the wheelbarrow," Mick said. "I put one in the ground and one in the air."

"Who in the Sam Hill are you?"

"Deputy Hardin, Eldridge County. I'm going to move my right hand real slow to show my badge."

Mick held it up and the man squinted.

"Come a little closer," the man said. "I can't hardly see the damn thing."

Mick nodded and eased forward slowly, holding the badge at the man's eye level.

"I got deputized yesterday," Mick said.

"Then pin the badge to your shirt or hook it on your belt before somebody shoots you down."

"You're right, Mr. Caldwell. I should'a done that already."

"What do you want my boy for?"

"I don't. I'm trying to find his ex-wife."

"Penny? She's up in Michigan."

Mr. Caldwell withdrew his rifle through the window, opened the door, and stepped to the grass. He held the weapon loosely, barrel aimed down.

"Don't you move," he said.

Mick nodded, watching the man sidestep across the yard and glance at the bullet hole in the wheelbarrow.

"That part's true," Mr. Caldwell said. "Randy, what happened here?"

"My gun went off on accident."

"That don't hardly ever happen."

"Well, it did, Daddy."

Mr. Caldwell looked at Mick for confirmation.

184

"He had one in the chamber," Mick said.

"You make him drop it?"

Mick nodded.

"Shotgun, too?"

Mick nodded.

"Shit fire, Randy. He took two guns off you and you shot the wheelbarrow?"

Randy shrugged and looked at the dirt. His father began laughing, a chuckle that blossomed. His laughter faded into the silence brought on by gunfire. He looked at Mick.

"What kind of lawman are you?" he said.

"Lucky."

"I reckon so," Mr. Caldwell said. "When I was a young feller, I shot a man's tires out. The sheriff asked me if I did it. I said no. He asked me what happened. I told him a bullet must have been laying in the road and the man ran over it."

He laughed again. Mick nodded.

"Way I see it," Mr. Caldwell said, "you and the county owe us a wheelbarrow."

Mick pulled out his wallet, extracted a hundred dollars, and offered it.

"Give it to him," Mr. Caldwell said.

Mick went to Randy, who took the money and counted it.

"Didn't cost that much," Randy said. "You want change?"

185

"No, get a better one," Mick said. "Where'd Penny go in Michigan?"

"I gave her my word I wouldn't tell nobody."

"Well, I didn't," Mr. Caldwell said. "She's got people up in Ypsilanti. Supposed to be by Detroit."

"Thank you," Mick said.

"Don't come on this property again unless you got a better reason than chasing down a man's ex-wife."

Mick nodded.

"I mean it," Mr. Caldwell said. "I'll do more than put bullets in the road next time."

"Yes, sir. I believe you. You mind if I get my pistol?"

Mr. Caldwell lifted the rifle.

"Go on and get it," he said. "Then drive on out of here."

Moving with care while keeping Mr. Caldwell in sight, Mick picked up his gun and held it away from him. He went to his truck, got in, and drove away. At the main road he stopped to wipe dirt and grass from the Beretta. He put the truck in gear and headed for town.

CHAPTER FOURTEEN

Mick parked at the hospital and crossed the lot beside a new two-story structure. It was dark brown with brown shutters, a brown roof, gutters, and downspouts. He assumed it was a medical facility. Most of them were shades of brown, as if someone had mandated the blandest possible color to offset the suffering that brought people there.

Shifty Kissick dozed beside Linda's bed, awaking when Mick pushed open the door. Linda lay on her back leashed to machines, the soft prongs of an oxygen tube askew below her nose.

"How is she?" Mick said.

"Doctor said good. I reckon she'd be a whole lot better if somebody didn't come in every hour and poke at her."

Mick nodded.

"I need a cigarette," Shifty said. "Be back in a minute."

"Anybody else been in?"

187

"Chief of police but the docs made him leave. I was glad. I never liked him as a boy and now he's a damn grown man cop."

"So am I, Mrs. Kissick."

"Well, I didn't know you when you were little."

"Johnny Boy come by?"

"No," Shifty said. "Ray-Ray and J.C. will after their lunch stuff is done."

"You get along with J.C.?"

"Lord, I do. He treats me like I'm a real good mother, which is a whole lot more than my sons ever did."

She rose and left. The sound of the closing door woke Linda, who blinked repeatedly, looked around as if ascertaining her whereabouts, and settled her gaze on Mick.

"Catch him yet?" she said in a raspy whisper.

"No. You remember anything?"

"Going across the yard. A gunshot. I ran in the house. Then nothing. Not a damn thing."

"Anyone in the house?"

"Maybe," she said. "I can't remember."

"We found a man dead. Shot."

"Was it me?"

"I don't know."

Mick watched the brief surge of energy leave her body. The muscles in her neck

188

relaxed. She was asleep. Mick held her hand and shut his eyes. He awoke when Shifty returned, smelling of cigarette smoke and eating chips from a small bag. She offered him some. He shook his head and she held out a candy bar, which he waved away.

"They got a machine down there charges two dollars and fifty cents for everything it sells," she said. "It kept my damn change."

"Better than eating hospital food."

"I might finish off somebody's fruit cup."

"J.C.'ll bring you something to eat."

He stood to let her sit.

"When you find the lowlife who shot her," she said, "don't bring him in. Leave him lay and go to the house, hear?"

"Yes, ma'am."

Mick drove to the sheriff's office and called Sandra from the safety of the parking lot. He liked her — *like* like, he thought, as if he were a schoolboy. He'd only liked one other woman that way and now she was happily living with another man.

Sandra answered the phone.

"I can see your truck out the window," she said.

"Uh, yeah. I'm in a rush. Any word from ballistics?"

"Linda did not fire her weapon. They dug a forty-five slug out of a window frame in

Gowan's house."

"Probably went through his lungs first. You hear from Johnny Boy?"

"No. He's out chasing down bird fighters. Not answering his phone and not calling in. Probably deep in the hills."

"Will you give him a message for me?"

"Yes, Mick," she said. "That's part of my job."

"Uh, right. Tell him I'm going up to Detroit. Got a lead on who shot Linda."

"When will you be back?"

"Depends on how hard it is to track the guy down."

"Way it works," she said, "if you leave your jurisdiction, you're supposed to notify the local police."

"I don't plan on working with them."

"That doesn't sound good."

"Nothing does right now."

"Not even the sound of my voice?"

"Uh . . ."

He couldn't think of anything to say. It had been the same with his ex-wife. The only woman he could be himself around was Linda. He understood that Sandra was joking in a flirtatious way — a light tone, an unanswerable question — and he was expected to respond in kind. He despised chitchat, even on the phone, but had to say

190

something.

"I like your voice," he said.

"Hot diggity dog," she said. "A high compliment from Acting Deputy Hardin. Thank you."

"You're welcome," he said automatically.

"Stay in touch."

The phone made a noise that indicated she'd ended the call. He stared at it, then glanced through the windshield at the office window. The anti-glare glass reflected shadows from an ornamental ginkgo in the lot, a tree he'd never liked due to its smell. He tossed the phone on the bench seat and drove to his sister's house, where he rested for an hour, a state between sleep and wakefulness that mostly refreshed him. A cold shower finished the job.

He double-checked his duffel bag — spare clips and ammunition, a knife, battle dressings, and a plastic container of pills that included Aleve, Ritalin, and hydrocodone. A small pouch held a compass, rope, three burner phones, a poncho, a mess kit, and a portable GPS. These were his standard travel supplies in the army and he'd kept them. Tucked into a hidden pocket was the money he'd withdrawn on base. Cash had been useful in the desert for bribes and rewards. He doubted he'd need it in Detroit but he liked the precision of embarking on an operation with the same provisions every time. Knowing he was fully prepared allowed him to focus on his primary objective.

He took Old Flemingsburg Road to Maysville, got on the AA Highway, and made Cincinnati in a little over two hours. He gassed up and headed north on I-75. The old truck slowed his pace, which he didn't mind. Army vehicles were slower and he'd become accustomed to driving with the front part of his mind while the back circled around the parameters of his mission. In his phone were two Detroit contacts, both career criminals, one a long-term professional. The other man was street meat with a gun. His plan was simple — go there and call them both.

Four and a half hours later he reached the southern edge of Detroit, passing a massive lot filled with hundreds of RVs for sale. He wondered what kind of city encouraged departure by making it so handy. You could buy a drivable house and leave forever. Mick had been in Detroit two years ago and had spent most of his time at a cheap motel near the airport. He didn't know where his contacts lived and wanted something more central. The Clark Street exit took him to

Mexicantown, where he ate at Schmear's Deli. When he asked for a kosher menu the tattooed waitress gave him a squinty look and shook her head briefly. He ordered pastrami, potato salad, and hummus.

He'd developed a taste for kosher food while working with a member of the Israeli Security Services, a small woman who was expert with firearms and undefeated at jiu-jitsu. Mick had mentioned that Mossad was the most effective and feared intelligence agency in the world. She scoffed and said, "What Mossad is most effective at is making everyone think that."

Mick finished eating and drove east into Hubbard Farms and stopped at the Hotel Yorba, a rundown place with an old yellow sign at the corner of the building. Three young men stared openly at him, assessing his potential value and threat. He removed eighty dollars from his duffel bag, tucked the bills in his shirt pocket, and left the truck. He walked straight toward the men, knowing he was on their turf, a few square yards of pavement that belonged exclusively to them. They'd fight and die for it. From their perspective, any unknown vehicle already belonged to them.

Gauging body language, Mick recognized the alpha as the shortest, broad through the hips and shoulders, like a hod carrier or a home-run hitter. Mick approached him and stopped just beyond the man's personal space.

"My truck," Mick said. "I'd like to hire you men to guard it for me."

"Cost you," the alpha said.

"Twenty apiece. Plus an extra twenty for you."

The alpha hesitated long enough to save face in front of his young followers, then nodded. Mick gave him the money and turned away. The Hotel Yorba was a place that asked no questions of its occupants, several of whom reclined in the lobby like they were taking the waters at a dirty spa. The front desk man had a bald pate with long, thin hair that ran to his shoulders as if it were fleeing a blight on top of his head. Preoccupied by a ball game on an iPad, he barely looked at Mick, who paid cash, registered under a false name, and took the steps to his room on the fourth floor. It was a cubicle with peeling wallpaper, a thin mattress that passed for a bed, an end table on uneven legs, and a tilted lamp with a burnt-out bulb. He lay on his back with the Beretta at hand and put himself to sleep for two hours.

CHAPTER FIFTEEN

Mick rose, distributed cash in several pockets, and left the hotel with his duffel bag. The street alpha had dropped the truck's tailgate and was sitting on it. Mick saw no damage or sign of an attempt at entry.

"Good work," he said.

"Ain't nobody mess with us," the alpha said. "This is our house."

Mick nodded. He handed the man another sixty dollars.

"I might be back late. You see my truck tonight or tomorrow, keep an eye on it."

"Cool. How old is it?"

"It's a 'sixty-three. Math ain't my best."

"Fifty-nine years old," the alpha said with a tone of pride. "Numbers is my thing."

"You're lucky. The whole world is based on numbers."

The young man brightened under the praise and Mick got in his truck. Hiring potential thieves to guard his vehicle was an old tactic. The street crew found it flattering to be charged with responsibility, and it prevented any future confrontation.

Mick drove an ever-widening perimeter until he found a public park with a baseball field and a hockey rink. He parked beside a YMCA building and entered the park with his duffel bag. Making calls from a public space was another old tactic. If anyone was tracking his phone, they'd find the park, not him. He scrolled through the numbers for Vernon Armstrong.

Vernon had family in Kentucky but grew up in Detroit and worked for Charley Flowers, a professional criminal Mick had never met. The crackdown on OxyContin in the hills created a shortage and addicts simply shifted to heroin. Charley Flowers filled market demand by utilizing the old "hillbilly highway" to move smack into Appalachia. Three years ago Vernon and another man had lain in ambush for Mick at his grandfather's old cabin, a task that didn't go well for the attackers.

Vernon's phone was answered by a child, then a woman's voice came on.

"This is my daughter's phone," she said. "She's seven. Call again and you get the po-po up your ass."

Mick ended the call, thinking that the

Detroit area code must be running out of numbers and was recycling old ones. He had a number for Vernon's boss, Charley Flowers. They'd spoken once, briefly, when Mick was helping Raymond's mother out of a jam. A man answered.

"Who this?"

"Tell Charley Flowers it's Shifty Kissick's friend from Kentucky."

"Ain't no Charley here."

"Pass the message on. He knows who I am. I got a proposition for him."

The man hung up and Mick waited. Two African American men were playing chess on a low table with sixty-four squares etched into the surface. An old man with gray hair and white beard stubble was in a defensive position against a skinny kid whose clothes didn't fit. The kid took a bishop in the center of the board. The old man dropped his chin in a nearly imperceptible nod to himself.

"Sure about that move?" he said.

"Hell, yeah," the kid said. "You're off the black diagonal and your queen's blocked. My rook is coming for you."

Three moves later the old man put the kid in checkmate.

"Shit," the kid said.

"You worried about my queen and forgot

197

about my knights. They hopping around out there like rabbits."

"Play again?"

"Pay up."

The kid placed four cigarettes on the table and began lining the pieces up for another game. The old man stared at Mick.

"You play?"

"Not against you, sir. You'd skunk me bad."

Mick's phone rang and he answered.

"What?"

"Give me something to prove you're who you say."

"Freddie had a stroke. Vernon's new partner shoots left-handed."

"Lot of folks know all that."

"Plastic garbage bag in the cell-phone lot."

The call ended. Mick moved away from the chess players. The scent of marijuana drifted on a breeze along with the sound of a tractor-trailer accelerating. Two skater kids did board slides on the low wall surrounding a dry fountain. His phone rang, the identifying number blocked.

"That you, army man?"

"I'm retired," Mick said.

"I ain't hiring. What do you want?"

"To meet."

"Why?"

"Something I need to talk to you about."

"So talk."

"Not on the phone," Mick said. "I can make it worth your time."

"Where you at?"

"Hang on."

Mick returned to the chess players, who told them the location.

"Clark Park," Mick said into the phone.

"No good."

"Tell me where to go."

"Alpine Street."

"What address?" Mick said.

"Get on the street. They'll find you. What are you driving?"

"Blue pickup. 1963 Chevy stepside."

"That's the first good thing you said."

"You like old trucks?"

"I don't like old anything. It means you ain't a Fed or an undercover motherfucker."

Charley Flowers hung up and Mick walked back to his truck. He plugged the street name into his phone GPS and took Clark to Michigan Avenue, then headed north on Livernois, a multilane street through a commercial area. Mostly it was businesses devoted to automobiles — parts, tires, body work, and muffler shops. One remarkably long building spanned three blocks with no signage. The side streets were residential. He turned onto Joy Street and drove past homes in various states of ongoing repair or equally ongoing disrepair. Churches, social service centers, and liquor stores. Boarded-up buildings with faded signs for used appliances and a restaurant called Annie Mae's Kitchen.

He turned onto Alpine. Originally a standard two-lane street, the cracked blacktop was lined with debris, dirt, and chunks of asphalt like blackened biscuits. Alpine was now a single lane with deep potholes and low block walls on both sides. Occasional patches of Virginia creeper draped the concrete wall, at the base of which grew Queen Anne's lace. He slowed for a T-intersection and the front of a car nosed out from Westfield Street. Mick stopped and the vehicle moved forward to block his path. It was an old police car, refurbished with high suspension and fat rims. Another vehicle pulled in behind Mick, a black SUV with windows dark as a hearse. It was a smart move, reminiscent of maneuvers he'd pulled in Iraq. He was trapped.

Mick held the Beretta across his lap and rolled his window down. A young man stepped from the police car holding an AR-15. Mick glanced in the rearview mirror and saw two men, one on each side of his truck, one black, one white, both armed. Mick left the gun in his lap and placed both hands on the window frame. The man approaching his window had dark skin, and a Lions hat cocked sideways. He held a nine-millimeter pistol aimed at Mick's head.

"Gun?" the man said.

Mick nodded.

"Slow."

Holding the Beretta between thumb and forefinger, Mick passed it out the window.

"Anything else?" the man said.

Mick shrugged and gestured to the duffel bag. The man waved to the car and a third man joined them, very short and very wide, as if he'd started out a giant, then got smashed down.

"Check the bag," the first man said.

The first man shifted position to prevent shooting his buddy in a crossfire. The short guy unzipped the bag and rifled through the contents, gave Mick a hard stare, then spoke.

"Knife, ammo. Bunch of other stuff."

"Take the bag," the first man said.

He stepped back and spoke to Mick.

"Get out slow. Leave the keys."

Mick eased from the truck and leaned against the hood for a pat-down search. Under guard, Mick got in the back seat of the black SUV. The driver watched him in the rearview mirror. The first man sat beside Mick, holding the pistol close to his body. This crew was good, Mick thought, trained. The one with the duffel bag sat in the front.

"What?" Mick said. "No hood?"

"Put your head between your knees. No more yak."

Mick did as he was told, trying to memorize the route, but lost track due to the jouncing over rough streets and a complex series of turns. The SUV stopped. The door opened.

"Get out," a new man said.

Mick left the vehicle and faced three armed men, two black and one white, all wearing loose clothing with heavy boots. There were no street signs and the neighborhood looked the same as Alpine Street. Mick stood before a large brick building beside an empty lot with three stripped cars tilted on their sides. It was a crude embattlement, ideal for defense.

The men force-marched him up a flight of stairs to a steel door. The lead man knocked a signal, stepped back, and stared at a tiny security camera in a corner. The door opened and Mick entered an antechamber where a different man passed a handheld metal detector over Mick. He told

Mick to remove his shirt and drop his trousers so they could check for a body wire.

Satisfied, he led Mick through a second steel door into a large room containing a luxury couch, a table, an armchair, and four chairs. Against one wall were state-of-the-art kitchen appliances. Two windows had steel shades partially raised to let in the thin Detroit sunlight. An M2 50-caliber Browning belt-fed machine gun mounted on a tripod was positioned to cover the exterior. It faced the open field he'd seen before. If the defensive position withdrew from the wrecked cars, the machine gun could protect the area.

The short man placed the duffel bag on the table and moved to the door. Mick stood calmly. He'd been in a similar position a dozen times before, waiting to meet a local warlord in Afghanistan. Some were psychopaths, some were brutal narcissists, and some were simply evil men. All participated in the tried-and-true method of intimidation by making Mick wait. The longer the wait, the crazier the strongman.

Three minutes later a door opened and in walked a light-skinned black man with short hair. A long scar bisected one eyebrow and ran down his cheek to the jawline. He wore a gray suit with a faint pattern, suitable for any occasion, and a light blue tie. Of average height and weight, he could be a man who worked in a bank, a middle manager for an office, or the owner of a real estate company — until the scar came into view. A stranger might assume it was from a car wreck but Mick knew different. The scar was too wide and slightly jagged, which meant no surgeon had sewn it.

The man looked at Mick for a long time. The confidence of assured power exuded from him like a scent.

"I'm Charley Flowers," he said.

"Mick Hardin."

Charley Flowers made a small gesture with his hands and everyone left the room except the man in the Lions hat.

"You met Bone already," he said. "Any fuss, Bone?"

Bone shook his head. Charley tipped his head to the duffel bag.

"What's in it?" Charley said.

"It's a bug-out bag," Bone said. "He came for war, ready to go black fast. He's trouble."

"Is that right, army man? Are you trouble?"

"Ex-army, Mr. Flowers. No, I'm not here for trouble."

"Then why the bag?"

"In case trouble comes my way."

"I like a man who's prepared. What do you want?"

"I have a small problem. Maybe you can help."

Mick watched amusement pass over Charley's face quick as a snake in the grass. He stared at Mick with fresh interest. Few people could resist curiosity about a small problem, especially from an adversary.

"Sit down," Charley said. "Do you want something to drink? I have a new espresso machine. La Marzocco. I love espresso."

"Thank you," Mick said. "Water's good."

He waited until Charley moved to the couch and indicated the upholstered chair. Mick sat. Bone busied himself with a bright yellow machine that emitted a tiny stream of espresso in less than a minute. He carried a small cup on a saucer to his boss, then brought Mick a bottle of expensive water.

"Nice setup," Mick said. "I guess you have a barracks, an armory, and a pantry with food for a month."

"Six months."

They sipped their drinks. Bone stood somewhere behind Mick. No outside sound penetrated the room and Mick wondered if the glass was bulletproof. He studied the window for a muzzle port.

"You approve of the fifty cal?" Charley said.

"Good weapon. I know the Barrett. Short barrel and lightweight for the field."

"Does it fire the seven-sixty-two round?"

Mick nodded. Charley sipped espresso with satisfaction and placed the cup on the saucer.

"Tell me," Charley said. "What kind of help do you need?"

"It's a family thing."

"Always tricky."

"Somebody shot my sister. She's in the hospital."

"Prognosis?"

"Six months of rehab and she can walk. Too soon to know if she'll limp, or how bad."

"Did it happen here in Detroit?"

"No, sir. In Kentucky."

"In that case, I'm not convinced I can do anything for you."

"I tracked down a witness," Mick said. "She came up here to hide. You got a guy working for you whose family is from the hills. Vernon Armstrong. He might know where to look."

"And if you find this witness, what then?"

"Ask her who shot my sister."

206

Charley leaned back with his espresso. He sipped it as if trying to make it last. Mick drank half his bottled water, oil to the machine of his body.

"I like a man who sticks by family," Charley said. "It's how I got my start."

Mick nodded.

"I was named for my uncle," Charley said. "He got zapped in Jersey fifty years ago. The killer was already dead, but not the man who gave the order. He retired to Florida."

"Florida's nice."

"Not for him," Charley said.

Mick amended his initial assessment. Charley Flowers was that rare sociopath in possession of charisma, ambition, cunning, and high intelligence. People like him excelled in the vicious arenas of politics and corporate warfare.

"Mr. Flowers," he said, "you strike me as a smart man."

"MBA from Ross down in Ann Arbor. And you?"

"Night school for eight years."

"That takes a certain discipline."

Mick nodded.

"If I help you with your problem," Charley said, "what's in it for me?"

"About eighteen thousand dollars. It's in the bag."

The same flicker of private amusement flitted across Charley's face. He set the tiny saucer on the burnished coffee table.

"I don't like to disappoint my guests," Charley said, "but I assure you that amount of money is more nuisance than anything else."

"You can't use cash?"

"Storage is the first problem. Next is transforming it into legal income."

"Laundering it."

"I prefer the term 'recycling.' Your eighteen becomes seven, which doesn't cover my daily outlay. Not worth it, I'm afraid."

"If you're negotiating," Mick said, "I can't go higher."

"When I was ten," Charley said, "I saved money for three months and bought a chameleon. A dark green one, about six inches long. I took it to the alley beside the pet store and set it down on white paper. I stood there thirty minutes. It never changed color. I put the chameleon on a piece of black tar paper. It stayed the same color. I stomped it with my Timbs."

Mick nodded.

"You know why I told you that story?" Charley said.

"You don't like lizards."

"It was an important day for me. I quit

wanting to fit in. I just killed anything that didn't do what I wanted."

Charley seemed to have something on his mind and Mick wondered what it was. If it was killing him, he'd already be dead. Maybe it was merely conversation with someone other than a minion or a rival. The most powerful people were often the loneliest.

"I'd still like to talk to your man Vernon," Mick said.

"You'll owe me one."

"One what?"

"A favor. Whatever I want, whenever I want."

"Agreed."

Charley looked at Bone, who stepped away, pulled out a cell phone, and spoke quietly. He ended the call.

"Ten minutes," Bone said.

"Do you mind waiting?" Charley said.

"No, sir," Mick said.

"A lot can happen in ten minutes."

"In Vegas you can get married or divorced."

"In twenty," Charley said, "you could do both."

Charley walked to the window as if surveilling his empire, a lone king in a land he'd taken by cunning and force. Mick understood that he was deliberately exposing his back to demonstrate how little he feared Mick.

"Here in Michigan," Charley said, "a lot of veterans become correctional officers. You ever think about it?"

"Not me. I'm done taking orders."

"Know any prison guards?"

"No, there's only one prison in the hills. It's in West Liberty with a street address of Road to Justice."

"A terrible irony," Charley said. "How about inmates? Know any?"

"I was gone twenty years. Why?"

"I'm thinking about the favor you owe me. There's no banking regulations in prisons. That means the Treasury Department can't access transactions or amounts. Makes it simple to recycle money. How much, Bone?"

"Six hundred thousand total," Bone said.

"Where?"

"Marquette, Baldwin, and Milan."

"How do you get your money back from a prison?" Mick said.

"We deposit it in the accounts of short-timers. They get released and sign the check to us. Bingo! Legitimate income."

"Smart," Mick said. "But I don't know any inmates or guards."

Bone spoke into his phone, then looked at Charley, who made a small gesture that Mick interpreted as confirmation. Bone spoke again. The entry door opened and Vernon Armstrong stepped in. He stood in a formal fashion, facing Charley Flowers.

"Boss," he said.

"You know this man?" Charley said, indicating Mick.

"Wish I didn't," Vernon said.

"You'll do what he wants," Charley said. "Drive him around. Let people know he's under my protection."

Vernon dropped his chin in assent. Charley dismissed him with a delicate gesture, then looked at Mick for several seconds. Mick realized he was seeing the true Charley Flowers, frigid eyes filled with ruthless fury.

"When I call in my favor," Charley said, "think about that chameleon."

CHAPTER SIXTEEN

Vernon's car was a late-model gray Impala with pristine surfaces. Mick put the duffel bag in the back seat.

"Figured you'd have a slicker rig," Mick said.

"Charley makes us all drive these. It's the commonest car in Detroit. Easier to blend in."

"Smart."

"Buddy, you don't know. Charley studies every angle and statistic before doing anything. He did the same with you or you'd not be here now."

Mick nodded. They got in the Impala and Vernon started it, blasting them with cold air and raucous music. He turned down the volume.

"Charley said drive you," Vernon said. "Where to?"

"I'm looking for a woman named Penny Lawson. She's from back in the hills. She came up here to stay with family. Maybe in Ypsilanti."

"That's about a forty-five-minute drive."

Vernon put the car in gear and drove slowly, veering around the worst areas of the street. He got on Southfield Freeway through a residential area. Forty-five minutes was sufficient time for Mick to nap. He tilted his seat back, closed his eyes, and spoke.

"Don't wreck me."

He awoke briefly when Vernon got on I-94 heading east, then slid into a solid REM state for a few minutes, becoming suddenly alert as the car exited the interstate for Huron Street. They entered a neighborhood of solid midwestern homes built to withstand winter, with narrow porches, low gables, and lap siding.

"You still with that guy who shoots southpaw?" Mick said.

"No. He got put away."

"Here in Michigan?"

"Federal system. Every few months they move him to fuck with his family. He was two weeks in a prison van going to Indiana."

"What'd they get him on?"

"Profiled him for an air freshener hanging off his rearview mirror. Then they found his guns. Ex-con, you know. Back in for another bid."

"You didn't get a new partner?"

"Naw, Charley's got me breaking in new guys."

"He must trust you."

"Enough to drive your ass around. Not a job I want, either."

Vernon made a turn onto Michigan Avenue and Mick wondered if it was the same one that ran through Detroit. A pretty long street. Vernon pointed to a tall stone structure shaped like a giant phallus with two flags at its base.

"See that?" Vernon said. "They call it 'the brick dick.' It's a water tower."

"Why the Greek flag?"

"Ypsilanti is Greek. Lot of history here if you know where to look. Ever hear of a town called Novi?"

"No."

"It's fancy now. Used to be nothing but a stop for the number six train. That's how it got its name. Get it?"

Mick shook his head.

"Number six in Roman numerals," Vernon said. "The signs all said 'No. VI.' Novi."

They drove deeper into the neighborhoods, past car lots, tattoo shops, and minimarts that sold gas and snacks. The buildings were lower to the earth, squat and wide like sumo wrestlers. Each street included a handy U-turn lane every mile or so.

"Where we headed?" Mick said.

"Mack's Place. It's a bar. Know anything about Ypsi?"

"Never been here."

"It's where all the families moved to when they came up for factory jobs. So many people from the hills, they call it 'Ypsitucky.' A lot of folks don't like that now. It's like a bad word."

"A bad word?"

"Yeah, it's dumb. There's a whole lot worse things to call somebody than being from Ypsitucky."

Vernon drove through a semi-industrial area that opened to a series of commercial strips — discount stores, pawnshops, payday loan shops, and churches. He stopped at a corner and got out. Jutting on struts from a brick wall was an old metal sign that said MACK'S. The single window was behind metal bars with a long opening at the top to allow light inside. Dented sheet metal paneled the door.

"You got a gun?" Vernon said.

"Yeah."

"In here if you don't, they'll give you one."

Mick nodded and followed him inside.

Sunlight outlined their silhouettes in a jagged shape along a stained floor, the shadow dissipating as the door closed behind them. Vernon stepped into the gloom while Mick stood still, allowing his pupils to expand and adjust to the dim light. The air smelled of cigarette smoke, grilled hamburger, sweat, whiskey, and beer. A few unoccupied tables sat in the center.

Against the wall was a row of booths separated by tall wooden panels like an old speakeasy. The booths were empty except one where an older couple sat, the woman resting against the wall with her eyes closed. Across from her a man talked and gestured as if making firm points.

Three customers sat at the bar far enough apart to drink in peace. The wall behind them had been papered with a lush flocking of red and black, now faded to an indiscernible pattern. A menu offered a burger with or without cheese and two kinds of potato chips. An old Hamm's beer sign displayed a tent, a canoe, and a campfire that appeared to emit smoke. Mick watched as the electronic image slowly moved sideways to show a waterfall flowing into a river. He averted his eyes to prevent being mesmerized.

Vernon went to the middle of the bar, rapped an ashtray against the surface, and stood with the patience of a man waiting for a bus. From the shadowed rear of the tavern came the dull rumble of pool balls falling into the trough of a pay-table. As a young soldier, Mick had played hours of eight ball at similar tables — the cue ball slightly larger than the others to keep it in play if someone scratched. Mick walked to the back, passing Vernon, who stared at an open trapdoor in the floor. Mick figured the bartender was down there gathering supplies. He continued to the back, where a Stroh's beer light made of plastic hung above the pool table in a little alcove. Behind the table were restroom doors, with a hand-written sign between them that listed the rules:

MONEY BREAKS
CALL POCKET
ONE FOOT ON THE FLOOR
NO DRINKS ON THE TABLE
NO DOPE SMOKING

Two men in their mid-twenties watched a slightly older man lining up a shot. The cue ball was against the rail and the space was too tight to draw back the stick and not hit the wall. The shooter had opened the men's room door and propped it with his foot to give himself enough room. He stroked the cue ball smoothly, propelling it down the table to kiss a striped ball, which dropped in a corner pocket. When he moved for the next shot, the door shut behind him. He made two more stripes then missed a long bank shot and sat on a bench. The second man studied the lay of the solid-colored balls. Satisfied, he circled the table and leaned over for a shot.

The third man gave Mick a quick upthrust of his chin, a traditional acknowledgment from the hills.

"Play?" the man said.

"Naw," Mick said, laying on some accent. "You boys would pick me like a chicken."

"Where you from, buddy?"

"Eldridge County."

"Down by Pick County?"

Mick nodded.

"What're you doing in here?"

"Nothing," Mick said. "Just got in today."

"Straight up from the hills?"

"Army first."

"Arlow was in the army."

Mick glanced at the man sitting on a low bench. He had the light hair and ruddy complexion that was common in the hills. A loose short-sleeve shirt was unbuttoned over a T-shirt. He stared at Mick.

"I was in the Eighty-Second out of Bragg," Arlow said. "Three tours in Iraq."

"Death from Above," Mick said, quoting the motto of the Eighty-Second Airborne. "I was in the Hundred and First."

"What was it? 'Rendezvous with Duckshit?' "

Mick grinned at the play on the word "destiny."

"Put in your twenty and get out?" Arlow said.

Mick nodded.

"You didn't jump all that time," Arlow said. "Desk job?"

"Transferred to CID."

Arlow stood slowly. Upright, he was a big man with broad shoulders, narrow hips, and long legs.

"He's a fucking cop," Arlow said.

"Retired," Mick said.

"Once a cop, always a cop."

Mick sensed a sudden movement from his left. His training overcame the natural instinct to move away and he turned to the threat, carrying the fight to the enemy. The pool player was swinging the cue two-handed like a baseball bat. Mick ducked beneath its arc, hit the man in the throat, and kicked him between the legs. The man dropped. Mick caught the cue stick and spun to the first man, who was pulling a Glock from the back of his pants. Mick struck his elbow with the cue stick, using enough force to numb the arm but not quite break a bone. The Glock fell from his useless grip. Mick kicked the gun away and punched the man twice, the second blow landing on the sweet spot behind the ear. The man's head snapped sideways and he collapsed.

Mick turned to the ex-soldier facing him across the pool table. Arlow was grinning.

"Not bad," he said. "You warmed up now?"

Mick nodded.

"How you want to go?" Arlow said. "Fists and boots?"

"Sure. It's a little tight for a gunfight."

Very slowly, Arlow reached inside his loose shirt and removed a tan SIG Sauer P320. Modeled after standard army issue, it was a more compact firearm for civilians. Arlow placed it beside a dead gnat on the pool table.

"That gun any good?" Mick said.

"I like the M17. But this one's better for the street. Weighs less. You?"

Mick withdrew his Beretta.

"Knife?" Mick said.

With a grin of faux-shame, Arlow propped

a boot on the bench and pulled a fixed-blade tactical knife from a sheath. He set it on the table.

"You know any Lawsons?" Mick said. "From Kentucky?"

"Naw, I'm from Grand Rapids."

The first attacker had begun to recover and was trying to pull a pistol from a cargo pocket. Mick gave him a quick pop with the pool cue, not a fierce blow but strong enough to get his attention. The man stopped moving and Mick removed a compact Smith & Wesson nine-millimeter Shield from the pocket. The man spat at Mick but missed.

"Dumb place for your weapon," Mick said.

"Fuck you."

"It turned sideways in there, didn't it? You can't find the grip easy. If your pants slide down, the gun'll bang your knee. I know a guy who shot himself that way. Notched his peter."

The man sucked the inside of his mouth in preparation to spit again. Mick struck him with the fat end of the cue stick, a light tap on the jaw that dazed him. Mick faced Arlow and spoke.

"You should tell these boys a thing or two."

"Can't tell them nothing," Arlow said. "They ain't lived nowhere else and don't know how dumb they are."

"That's true all over."

From the entrance to the alcove came the unmistakable sound of a shotgun racking a shell into the chamber. Mick stopped moving, aware that he held a pistol in each hand.

"Boy," a man's firm voice said. "Put those fucking guns down."

Mick obeyed, placing the weapons carefully on the pool table. Very slowly he pivoted to face a man holding a Benelli combat shotgun. He was short and wide, built like a stump, with no neck, as if his head was clamped to his torso. His shoulders were broad and flat like the mantle of a fireplace. Behind him was Vernon, shaking his head at Mick.

"Take three steps back," the man said.

Mick did so. He was nearly against the wall and the guns were out of reach.

"Your place?" Mick said.

"Yeah, my goddamn place. Now get the fuck out of here."

"Wasn't him," Arlow said. "Joe Bob started it."

"I don't care who started what," the man with the shotgun said. "This shitbird sure as hell finished it. Now get out. You, too, Arlow."

"Uh," Vernon said. "He's with me."

"Then you're out, too. All y'all. Banned for a week."

"What I mean," Vernon said, "this guy's with me and you know who I'm with."

"Yes, I do."

"Well, then."

The armed man backstepped until he stood beside Vernon. Still holding the shotgun on Mick, he gave Vernon a quick glance.

"You saying he's one of Charley's guys?"

"Not exactly," Vernon said.

"Quit fucking around. What exactly?"

"I don't know. Charley told me to drive him."

"Told you personally?"

"That's right."

Mack gestured with the shotgun.

"Talk, shitbird," he said.

"I'm an associate of Mr. Flowers."

"What the hell does that mean?"

"We do each other favors," Mick said. "I apologize for the trouble in your place, Mr. Mack. I'll pay you for any damage."

"You can't hurt this goddamn place. Call me Shorty. Everyone does."

He lowered the shotgun fully and looked

at Arlow.

"Get your buddies out of here," Shorty said.

"He's a cop," Arlow said. "And they ain't my buddies."

"They are now. Drag their asses out the back. Vernon, you help him. Shitbird, come with me."

Arlow and Vernon looked at each other and shrugged in tandem, ready to work together and ease the other's load. They bent to the task. Shorty gathered the weapons and motioned for Mick to precede him into the main room. Four fresh cases of warm beer were stacked on the end of the bar.

"Need help with that beer?" Mick said.

"I don't need no goddamn help from nobody, leastways not you."

Mick nodded.

"Set your ass down," Shorty said. "What you got going with Charley is none of my goddamn business. But coming in here makes it mine."

Mick sat at the last booth. Shorty dragged a chair over and sat with the shotgun across his lap. He began unloading the pistols.

"That Benelli," Mick said, "it's the M1014, right?"

"Plenty of pew-pew. I got used to it in the sand."

"Most of the guys I knew that used them were marines."

"Semper fi. You?"

"Hundred and First."

"Goddamn army dog."

"You say 'goddamn' a lot. Anybody ever tell you that?"

"My ex-wife, yeah. Know why I do? I'll tell you. When I was a kid in Kentucky, saying 'god damn' was the worst of all. It was taking the Lord's name in vain. But I didn't hold with that. Somebody sneezed and folks said 'God bless you.' Right there's taking the Lord's name in vain if you ask me. Everybody sneezes and everybody cusses."

"Never thought about it that way," Mick said.

"Most don't. What do you want?"

"I'd like my Beretta back."

"Maybe in a minute. Why'd Vernon bring you here?"

"Somebody shot my sister. A witness came here to hide, a woman name of Penny Lawson."

"Don't know her. What's this about you being a cop?"

"Army CID. Retired."

"Shit fire," Shorty said. He grinned and

shook his head. "You'll not get nothing out of Arlow. He spent more time in the goddamn brig than the barracks."

"I don't care. I want to find Penny Lawson."

Vernon came in the front door with a disgusted expression, wiping his hands on his pants.

"The one boy puked," he said.

"In here?" Shorty said.

"No, the alley."

"Don't matter, then. Where they at?"

"In their car," Vernon said. "Arlow's asking for his knife. Says he carried it overseas."

"Why ain't he in here asking for it his ownself."

"You banned him."

Shorty's quick grin developed into a high-pitched laugh. He slapped his knee twice, something Mick hadn't seen anyone do in twenty years. If Corsica didn't work out, he could move up here. It was more like home than home. Shorty's laugh dwindled to a chuckle and he spoke.

"Tell him to come in here."

Vernon went to the door and waved Arlow in. The old couple had left but the regulars at the bar remained in their spots, ignoring everything but their drinks. Shorty carried the Benelli behind the bar and replenished

226

the glasses. Mick watched the perpetual waterfall on the Hamm's beer sign. The campfire continued to smoke. Nothing had happened there or ever would — just a perpetual flow of water and fire. Shorty returned.

"You like that sign?" he said.

"Ain't seen one before."

"It was my daddy's. This was his place. He worked the line at Ford. Got hurt on the job and used the insurance to open this joint. Had a man offer me two grand for that goddamn sign once."

Arlow came in and stayed ten feet from the table, reminding Mick of a house dog trying to show respect while humans ate a meal. Vernon stood a few feet away, enough to communicate the vestiges of his independence. It wasn't the shotgun they feared, it was Shorty's sheer force of will, his aura of command and control. Mick wondered what his job had been in the Corps.

"Arlow didn't do nothing back there," Mick said. "It was them other two."

"You and him," Shorty said, "looked like you was ready to go. Is that right, Arlow?"

"Yeah."

"So how come you're sticking up for each other now? Banding together against a marine?"

Arlow shrugged and glanced at Mick with an expression of chagrin.

"About the size of it," Mick said.

"Goddamn army dogs. You two still aiming to fight?"

"No," Mick said.

"Yeah," Arlow said.

"Well, then, what's it going to be?" Shorty said.

"He needs an ass-kicking," Arlow said.

Shorty shrugged and made a gesture for Mick to go ahead, as if inviting him to an all-you-can-eat buffet.

"In here?" Mick said.

"Yeah, shitbird," Shorty said, "but don't bust no glass. I already swept."

Mick stood and approached Arlow, who set himself — weight on his back foot, arms and fists in a boxer's stance. His right was a little low, which meant his midsection was vulnerable. Mick stuck his hand out as if to shake and moved closer.

"I'm game to let it go," he said.

"Nope," Arlow said.

Mick stepped in swiftly, and jabbed twice. Arlow pivoted to defend with his left. Mick ducked his swing, grabbed Arlow's shirt, jerked him forward, and head-butted Arlow's nose. He staggered and Mick delivered a hard left to his liver. Arlow's knees buckled and he collapsed, gasping.

Mick went back to the table and sat.

"Nice," Shorty said.

"Learned it from an SAS man. He'd always break a nose, but I went easy."

They watched Arlow's writhing subside as the pain faded. He lay curled on his side like a child sleeping, then stretched on his back, breathing long and slow. Vernon was careful to keep his eyes away from Mick. Two customers came in, saw Arlow on the filthy floor, and left.

"Damn, son," Shorty said to Mick. "You're costing me money."

"You could unban those guys. No harm done."

"Except to them."

"They made a dumb mistake is all."

"What if that Lawson woman makes a mistake?"

"I won't touch her. Just need information. But if she knows I'm here, she'll run."

Shorty's expression indicated that he understood and agreed. He leaned back in his chair. Mick waited for him to make a decision.

"You ain't the only one looking for a Lawson," Shorty said. "Young feller was in a few days ago, saying Hank Lawson owed him money. Wanted to know if he'd been in."

"Where's Hank live?" Mick said.

"I don't know. But that young feller will. I'll get hold of him."

"Why would you do that?"

"You ain't the only one who does favors with Charley Flowers."

Shorty gathered the unloaded ammunition, carried it behind the bar, and stashed it out of sight. Three young guys came in wearing sports jerseys and hats. They ordered shots and beer. Shorty checked on his regulars, who wanted refills. He topped off their drinks and made a series of phone calls.

Mick motioned for Vernon to join him at the table. Vernon stepped around Arlow and sat.

"You don't mess around, do you?" Vernon said. "What now?"

Mick shrugged. He wondered what it would be like to inherit a bar, to have a father who'd been a businessman. His own father drank like a fish which was why Mick tried to avoid liquor as much as possible.

Shorty came to the table without the shotgun.

"Charley's man vouched for both of you," he said. "You can have your guns back."

Arlow appeared to be taking a nap on the floor. His left hand twitched, reminding Mick of a sleeping dog. People said dogs dreamed but Mick didn't think so. Humans had a tendency to ladle their experience onto other people — emotions, motivations, and fears. They did the same with pets.

"You think dogs dream?" he said.

"Sure," Shorty said. "Food, sex, and barking at cars. Same as me."

"You bark at cars?" Vernon said.

"I've got half a mind to bark you right back into yours."

"Let me know when you get a whole mind," Vernon said.

"Don't get smart, son. You'll be laughing on the other side of your face when I'm done."

Shorty's cell phone rang like an old Model A car horn. He answered, listened, and hung up.

"Got a man coming," he said. "He owes me one. Now you do, too."

Mick nodded. He'd been in Detroit less than six hours and was already two favors deep, maybe three. He wondered how these people kept track of it all. Maybe the whole city was an intricate network of backscratching, coercion, and abetment. He preferred the army method of giving and taking

231

orders. The hill way was to help if you could, with no expectation of return. It was part of the reason Mick never got mad at people. The effort to remember who he was mad at wasn't worth the trouble.

Arlow rose from the floor, gave Mick a short nod, and left. Four more customers had entered, two black and two white. They sat in a booth discussing the players for the Steelers, Lions, and Pistons, as if the athletes were relatives with complex difficulties of great importance. It was noise to Mick, the soundtrack of men everywhere. The more unsatisfying their jobs and personal lives, the more passionate they were about a sports team.

A man in his thirties came into the tavern, wearing workman's clothes, boots, and a large red jacket. His light brown hair was tucked beneath a red cap with an emblem of a spoked wheel and a pair of wings. Mick figured it was some kind of race car hat. The man nodded to Shorty and swaggered to the table.

"Hey, Hollis. Still looking for Hank Lawson?" Shorty said.

"Sure am. He here?"

"No, but this man is hunting him, too."

Hollis narrowed his eyes at Mick in a hostile manner. Mick wondered if everyone in Detroit was tough or tried to come off that way. This guy could go either way.

"If Hank owes you money," Hollis said, "I'm first in line."

Mick shook his head.

"How much?" Shorty said.

"Four bills," Hollis said. "A signed Stevie Wonder jersey."

"Pretty cheap. Maybe he found out it was forged."

"No way. I got a certificate of authority and a hologram. Hank gave me half the money. Not my usual way but I needed it at the time. Now I want the rest."

Mick was puzzled but it didn't matter. People collected all kinds of things. Maybe a shirt was more rare than a signed record. As a Detroit guy, Stevie Wonder probably had laundry all over the city.

"If Hank ain't here," Hollis said, "what do you want me for?"

Shorty gestured to Mick.

"You check where Hank lives?" Mick said.

"Four fucking times. He ain't there."

"Was anybody?"

"Nobody answered the door."

"Hear anything inside?" Mick said.

"Yeah, TV. Sounded like cartoons or some shit."

"What's the address?"

"What do I get out of this?" Hollis said to Shorty.

"You and me are square from before," Shorty said.

"Ain't enough, man. Me coming down here squared us up. Now this fucker wants an address. I ain't getting mixed up in trouble."

"You missed all the trouble," Shorty said. "If you'd been here, you'd be minding your goddamn manners."

Hollis turned to face Mick and lifted his red jacket to expose a nine-millimeter pistol with dull grips.

"What are you going to do?" Hollis said. "Beat the address out of me? You best be strapped and bringing a lunch. You'll need both."

Shorty shook his head and began chuckling. Mick spoke in a calm and practical tone, as if contemplating items on a menu.

"Three ways to get information," he said. "Buy it, strong-arm it, or trade for it."

"Which one is on your mind?" Hollis said.

"Beating you down is a risk. You might get resentful and give me the wrong address. I don't have any Stevie Wonder records to trade. That leaves money."

Shorty's chuckle shifted to laughter and Vernon appeared amused.

"What?" Mick said.

Shorty pointed to a framed photograph behind the bar. A man held a large silver stovepipe over his head. He wore a white shirt bearing the race car emblem on Hollis's hat.

"That Stevie Wonder," Shorty said, "not the musician. Steve Yzerman. Stevie Y. Stevie Wonder. Greatest hockey player ever."

"What's that he's holding up?" Mick said.

"The fucking Stanley Cup, asshole," Hollis said.

Mick nodded and turned to Shorty.

"I'm getting tired of this boy," Mick said.

"Uh-huh," Shorty said. "He has that effect on folks."

"If you want some," Hollis said to Mick, "bring it on, fucker."

"Vernon," Mick said. "Would you mind standing up and moving back for a minute?"

Vernon stood, stepped behind his chair, and walked a few feet away.

"You ready?" Mick said.

Hollis moved his hand closer to his pistol. Mick slouched as if getting comfortable, shot his leg out, and kicked Vernon's empty chair. It slammed across the floor and struck Hollis. Mick sprang forward as if catapulted and snatched the pistol from Hollis's waistband. With his other hand Mick slapped

235

Hollis twice in the face.

"What's the address?" Mick said.

"You said something about buying information."

Mick cocked his head, grinning. He was starting to like these Detroit guys. Not a one had backed down.

"Vernon," Mick said. "Give him two hundred bucks."

Vernon pulled a slender wallet from his front pocket, no more than a band of leather with a metal clip. A credit card was visible and a sheaf of bills.

"Four hundred," Hollis said.

Shorty began laughing again. Mick nodded, grinning.

"All right," he said. "Four hundred. But it'll cost you two to get your gun back."

Hollis poked his bottom lip out, frowned, and shrugged.

"Okay," he said.

Vernon gave him the cash and Hollis recited the address of Hank Lawson. Mick removed the clip and set the gun on the table.

"I need that clip, man," Hollis said. "The street knows I carry cash."

"You should keep that in mind when you negotiate."

"Shorty," Hollis said. "Can I rent a gun

236

off you?"

"Get out of here," Shorty said.

Hollis shrugged, retrieved the empty pistol, and left with a more pronounced swagger than when he'd come in.

"Is the whole city like this?" Mick said. "Or just your place?"

"Little of both," Shorty said. "Hollis has more balls than a pool table."

"I owe you for damages?"

"Naw, shitbird. Next time you come in, let me know in advance. I'll sell tickets and make a goddamn fortune."

Shorty returned their guns. Mick followed Vernon to his car and gave him two hundred dollars from his duffel bag. Vernon entered the Lawson address into his cell phone GPS.

CHAPTER SEVENTEEN

Vernon drove away from Mack's Place into a more residential area of Ypsilanti. Grand old houses from the 1920s gave way to modest mid-century homes, with a few apartment buildings scattered about. Smaller trees indicated cheaper housing, as if poor people deserved less shade. Vernon stopped at a corner.

"This the street," he said. "Down here on the right."

"Cruise it at normal speed. Go to the corner, turn, and park."

Vernon drove while Mick surreptitiously reconned the street. There were no sidewalks. A few driveways had free-standing basketball hoops anchored by sandbags. The Lawson house was nondescript — yard neatly mowed, shrubs trimmed, a metal shed on the side, no cars in front. Vernon stopped as instructed.

"What now?" he said.

"I'm going in. Drive around the block and park near the house. Wait for me. If you hear gunfire, give me two minutes. If I'm not out by then, leave."

Mick left the car and strolled along the curb as if visiting a neighbor. He walked past the house and pretended to consult his phone, then turned around and went to the front door. He heard the sound of a TV. The door was locked. He circled the house, ducking below the windows, and entered the backyard. The only fence was a tall wooden one in the rear. The house had a small deck in back, with a charcoal grill and four rusty chairs. He inserted his knife between the screen-door frame and the jamb, and gently lifted the blade to release the hook lock. The back door was locked as well. He was out of options, an off-duty deputy far from his jurisdiction, but information about his sister's shooter was inside. He stepped back and glanced around, seeing nobody. He took a breath, kicked the door open, and charged inside.

A kitchen led to an empty living room with a TV at low volume. He moved down a short hall past a bathroom. At the end of the hall a door opened and a woman stood with a can of mace aimed at him. The left side of her face was swollen from dark bruising. Two Band-Aids covered a wound above her eye. Mick opened his hands and spread his arms at his waist. The slow gesture was modeled after a painting of the Virgin Mary he'd seen in Italy. It had saved him before and might do so now.

"You're hurt," he said. "I want to help."

"Get out," she said.

Mick nodded and took a step back. From behind her in the room came a child's voice.

"Uncle Hank?"

"No, honey," the woman said. "Stay back."

"I want to see Uncle Hank!"

The mace wavered in the woman's hand as she glanced into the room.

"You're Penny Lawson," Mick said.

"How'd you find me?" she said.

"Somebody knew Hank."

"He ain't here."

"It's not him I'm looking for. I came to talk to you, Penny. I need your help. It's about my sister back in Eldridge County."

"Mama?" the child said.

The woman lowered the mace as if hiding it from the child and shifted her body toward the room beside her.

"Mama, I'm scared."

Penny entered the room and Mick followed her to the doorway. Sitting on a bed was a child of eight or nine holding a stuffed

240

bear and a book like she was reading to her toy. An expression of fear passed over her face as Mick stepped out of view.

"Penny," he said, "I'm sorry I scared your daughter. I just need to talk a minute. How about I wait in the front room on you."

Mick went down the hall to the living room. Flickering across the TV screen were images of a kids' show that featured a mermaid and a talking submarine. On the coffee table were a bowl of crackers and several books for children. Facing the TV was a large easy chair with a built-in cooler and a magazine rack. The curtains were drawn. A chain lock secured the front door.

Penny entered the room with a cell phone and the mace.

"I apologize for busting in on you," Mick said. "I knocked and heard the TV and went around back."

"I push this button and it's 911."

Mick nodded.

"You're smart," he said. "You're protecting your daughter. I don't think you'll make that call because you don't want the law up in here. They'll find out what happened back home and take you into custody. Your daughter will go into temporary foster care. I know you don't want that. You're a good mother. I want to help you."

Penny stood as if immobilized except for facial tics. She embodied a combination of ferocity and sorrow, a forlorn strength. Mick had seen it before in people who realized there was no way out. She'd come here to escape. Now that she was found, she had nowhere else to go. She wanted to deny the situation but was forced to accept it for her daughter's sake.

"Let me help you," he said.

She lowered the cell phone and leaned against the doorjamb.

"Let's sit down," he said. "Then you can tell me what happened."

She moved to the couch and eased into it as if deeply fatigued. Mick sat on the ottoman, ensuring that his head and shoulders were below hers, reducing his authority. He'd have to look up to talk to her, focus on the undamaged eye.

"Leo do that to you?" he said.

Penny stared at her lap and nodded.

"First time?" he said.

She shook her head to indicate no.

"I can take you to a doctor."

She shook her head again.

"What would you like?" he said. "What do you want?"

She looked at him as if no one had ever asked her that before.

"I don't know," she said. "I used to but not no more."

"You want your daughter safe and she is now. You want to be safe from Leo and you are."

"Why are you here?" she said.

"My sister is the sheriff of Eldridge County. Somebody shot her. They killed your boyfriend, too. I'm trying to find out what happened. Was somebody else there?"

She shook her head, blinked rapidly, and glanced away.

"How is she?" Penny said. "Your sister."

"In the hospital but she'll be all right."

She nodded as if relieved.

"Is it possible," Mick said, "that your daughter saw Leo hit you? Maybe you promised yourself you would never let her see that again. Maybe he did and you did something to stop it. Is that possible?"

Penny stared at him with a surprised expression.

"What happened?" Mick said.

"He hit me. Then hit Hannah. She ran in the back and I shot him."

"Where did you shoot him?"

She tapped her chest.

"How many times?"

"Just once. He fell down."

"What'd you do then?"

"I went to get Hannah. Then the door busted open and somebody came in with a gun. I didn't know who it was. I saw the uniform after."

"After what, Penny?"

"After I shot her. I'm sorry. I thought it was somebody else trying to hurt us. I didn't know she was a cop. I'm so sorry."

"You shot Leo, then went to get Hannah. Is that right?"

"Yes."

"Did you carry the gun with you? When you went to Hannah?"

"No. I set it down. I didn't have it."

"Then what?"

"I got Hannah and some of her stuff. She has a little backpack."

"Where were you when my sister came in?"

"In the living room."

"With Hannah?"

"No. Yes. She was with me."

"Where was the gun?"

"The gun? On the couch. No, the coffee table."

"Were you sitting down?"

"No, I was standing. In front of the couch. The door banged open. I picked the gun up and shot."

Mick nodded. The explanation was both

better and worse than he'd expected. Better because it wasn't deliberate. Worse because Penny was lying.

"Where was Hannah?" he said.

"Back in her bedroom."

"You said she was with you in the living room. With her backpack."

"No," she yelled. "No. She was never up front. She was in her bedroom the whole time. I'm so sorry."

"I know," he said. "I understand."

"Then why do you keep asking me?"

"Because my sister was shot in the leg below the knee. If you had done it, the angle of entry would have been a hard slant. But it wasn't. The bullet entered my sister's leg at a perpendicular."

"I don't know what all that means."

"It means you didn't shoot my sister. It means somebody else did. Somebody short and sitting on the couch. Somebody you're trying to protect."

He watched her face cycle rapidly through expressions, hardening and tightening, eyes wide, pupils dilated. Her mouth twitched, then the skin below her eyes. Her body was immobile.

"Where's the gun?" he said gently.

"In the bedroom closet. What's your sister's name?"

"Linda."

"That's a pretty name."

Mick nodded.

"It's German," he said. "Means soft and tender, which she's anything but. She's tough like you."

"I'm not," Penny said.

"People never know until they have to be."

From the bedroom down the hall they heard Hannah's voice.

"Mama! I'm thirsty!"

Mick stood and went to the front door.

"I have to go outside for a minute. I'll be right back. Don't worry, nothing will happen. I want to help you."

He unlocked the door, went out, and crossed the street to Vernon's car. Vernon rolled the window down.

"No luck?" he said.

Mick opened the rear door and removed his duffel bag.

"A few more minutes," he said.

Vernon rolled the window up. Mick returned to the house and sat on the ottoman with the bag on his lap. He could hear Penny talking to her daughter down the hall. Hannah laughed and he marveled at the child's resiliency.

Penny came back to the front room and remained standing, looking at the bag with mistrust. She flinched when Mick unzipped it. He pulled out nine banded packets of currency and set them on the coffee table.

"This money's for you," he said.

"What are you, a drug dealer?"

"No, I travel with cash for emergencies."

"I can't take your money."

"I have a job and a pension. I don't really need this. You can use it to leave Detroit."

"Why?"

"You can't stay here."

"No, I mean why are you doing this?"

"Leo's got family, right?" Mick said.

"Big bunch of brothers and I don't know how many cousins."

"They'll be looking for you. I found you in four days. Do you understand what I'm saying?"

She nodded rapidly.

"Leo abused his ex-wife, Carla Jo. I talked to her. He hit you then Hannah. You shot him to protect yourself. Hannah shot my sister to protect you. Now I'm trying to help you. This is eighteen thousand dollars."

Penny nodded again, her face taut.

"Use some to get out of town. Save the rest for Hannah. She'll need to talk to somebody."

"She doesn't remember anything. None of it."

"She will," Mick said. "It's in her somewhere. She'll need professional help. Use the rest of the money then."

"Go where? I don't know anybody anywhere but here."

"That's good. Tell Hank you're moving to Seattle then go somewhere else. Get a job working for cash. Waitress or cleaning hotels. Something like that. Did you drive your own car up here?"

She nodded.

"Sell it and buy another one before you leave."

She nodded again.

"One more thing," he said. "I need Leo's gun."

"What? Why?"

"Possession of the weapon puts you in the thick of it. I'll get rid of it. Please, go get the gun."

She walked down the hall, spoke to her daughter, and returned carrying a paper sack from the IGA in Rocksalt. She set it on the coffee table. Mick looked inside then placed the sack in the duffel bag. He handed her a burner phone.

"Throw away your phone and use this one," he said. "Don't call anybody you know. Nobody. Do you have shared custody of Hannah?"

"No, it's just me."

"Good. Randy won't have a legal reason to track you."

"You know Randy?"

"We met."

"How do you know so much about this?" she said.

"I used to be an army cop."

"Not no more?"

"I don't know what I am any more, Penny."

He picked up the duffel bag and moved to the door.

"Hey," she said. "Thanks."

Mick nodded and left. He walked quickly to the car, tossed the duffel bag in the back, and got in the passenger seat.

"Where to now?" Vernon said.

"My truck."

"You hungry? There's a good Coney up here."

"Truck. No more talk."

Vernon shrugged and drove back to Detroit. Mick wondered if he'd done the right thing. He ran through his thinking, checking the logic of his instinct. If Penny got arrested here, she'd be extradited to Kentucky, where she'd take the rap for Leo and Linda both. She could make a plea deal and serve prison time or go to trial. Either option left her at risk of retribution from Leo's family. Regardless, the kid's life would be traumatized worse and she'd probably wind up living with her father in the trailer by the river. Yes, he concluded, he'd done the right thing by helping Penny.

Vernon drove slowly along Alpine Street to avoid the potholes. A guard materialized from the shadow of a rusted steel overhang. Vernon stopped, waved, and waited, then told Mick he was cleared to leave. Mick opened the door.

"Give Charley a message for me," he said. "Tell him I owe him one."

Returning to his role as gangster, Vernon stared straight ahead without speaking. Mick got in his truck and headed south. Once clear of Detroit, he stopped for gas and called Johnny Boy, who didn't answer. He tried Sandra, who told him Linda was awake and doing well. Shifty was still there, spelled every few hours by Ray-Ray and J.C.

During the drive to Kentucky he speculated about his current life if he'd married Penny. She was tough, loyal, and resourceful. Maybe he'd still be married. Then again, his ex-wife Peggy shared the same traits. So did Sandra. It wasn't the women, he realized, it was him. He preferred being alone, in motion, or both. He'd have fucked things up with Penny but at least she wouldn't have killed anyone.

CHAPTER EIGHTEEN

Johnny Boy sat in his office, upset by all and sundry. He'd sorted through five plastic bags of garbage, examining each item and putting it in a fresh bag. He didn't find a gun and his uniform was stained from rotten food, mud, and unknown liquid. The station had no storage room, only a single closet for supplies and cleaning equipment. He put the bags in Linda's office. Sandra watched him without comment and he wondered if it was due to his new status as sheriff or a case of silent judgment. He was spinning his wheels at best.

He sat at his desk and studied multiple index cards on which he'd written what he knew. Johnny Boy was a methodical and organized thinker but had always relied on others to give him instructions. Now he had to do it on his own. He didn't like it but there was no choice — he was the damn sheriff — and he studied the information again and again.

Linda was shot by a pistol.

Leo was killed by a pistol.

Linda had not fired her service weapon.

Pete Lowe and Hack Darvis were killed with a shotgun.

Roscoe Reeder was living in a chicken house with Pete Lowe's three-thousand-dollar rooster.

Footprints behind Hack's place were from a size-seven shoe made by Iris.

A refrigerator in Hack's shed contained a jar of what was probably snake poison.

The only links Johnny Boy saw were roosters and guns. With Mick in Detroit chasing a witness to Linda's shooting, Johnny Boy decided to limit his investigation to Pete Lowe and Hack Darvis. He rearranged the index cards and read through them again as slowly as he could, which was easy because there was so little information. He didn't have murder weapons or fingerprints. The only potential evidence was a snake in a box stored at his cousin Caney's house. The name Caney Rodale bounced around in his mind.

Abruptly Johnny Boy stood, shoving his roller chair behind him against the row of filing cabinets that lined the wall. He went straight to the correct cabinet, opened the third drawer down for the letter *r,* and withdrew a file for Billy Rodale, an unsolved homicide from 1997. It was partly typed but mostly hand-written by the former sheriff, Troy Johnson, in a kind of personal shorthand. Rodale had been shot to death in his home. The suspect list had nine names, as if Rodale had made enemies hand over fist. Some were crossed out, then added again. At the bottom, written in pencil, was the name Virgil Caudill.

Sandra immediately looked up as Johnny Boy emerged from his office.

"Going to the DMV," he said. "Any word on Linda?"

"She's getting better. Ray-Ray's mom is there. I'm going over when I'm done."

"How about Mick?"

"Still in Michigan, far as I know. Before that he called twice to get addresses in Farmers and Sharkey."

Johnny Boy left. Temporarily obsessed with his task, he neglected to recognize the inherent joy of driving the official sheriff's vehicle. It smelled of the chemicals used to clean Linda's blood. He parked in the DMV lot and entered a room where hard plastic chairs were bolted to the floor as if to maximize the discomfort of anyone sitting. Several people waited, each clutching a small piece of paper with a number on it. A few were teenagers, exuberant about their impending futures. The rest had a birthday during the current month. Johnny Boy vaguely wondered if there was an optimal birth month to reduce the waiting time. He'd heard more babies were born in August because it was nine months after the first cold snap.

He went to the clerk's window, where a woman he'd known all his life presided over her domain. She ignored him. Not so much Johnny Boy himself, but the presence of a human who'd arrived without his number being called.

"Mrs. Flannery," Johnny Boy said.

She waved her hand briefly without glancing from her computer screen. The gesture reminded him of someone making a futile attempt to ward off flies at a church picnic. She wore a sleeveless gray dress under which was a long-sleeve white shirt. Her long hair was pulled to the top of her head by a hair clip, creating the effect of an elongated skull that tapered up.

"Mrs. Flannery," he said again. "This is official business."

She completed a few more pecks on the keyboard before lifting her head. Her vision followed in a reluctant manner.

255

"Johnny Boy!" she said. "It's nice to see you. You're with the police now?"

"No, ma'am. I'm the sheriff."

"Ain't it still yet that Hardin girl?"

"She got hurt. So it's me till she's better."

She blinked with a puzzled expression.

"I was deputy before," he said. "I'm filling in till Linda's back."

"Oh my stars," she said. "I remember when I gave you your first driver's license. And now you're the sheriff. It just goes to show you. Sure does."

"Yes, ma'am. I need a little help. I'd like to get a copy of a driver's license from the '90s. Virgil Caudill."

"I knew his mom and sister. They're gone now. So many young people move away. All my kids did. But you stayed to be the sheriff!"

"Could you please get me a copy of Virgil's driver's license. High a quality as you have. I need to see the picture on it."

"A color copy costs more. On account of the ink."

"That's all right. Charge it to the county."

"Right, right. The sheriff's office!"

She returned her attention to the computer. As she worked she made small sighs and grunts, moving back in time among electronic files. She used her phone to

256

request delivery of a document.

"Be just a minute," she said. "Color printer, it's way back yonder and I can't leave my post. You know how that goes, right, Sheriff?"

"Yes, ma'am."

Five minutes later he carried a copy of Virgil's photo outside and inspected it in the sunlight. He concentrated on the face above the nose. Still unconvinced he returned to the sheriff's office and asked Sandra if they had access to facial software that would age a photograph.

"Use your phone," she said. "There's an app."

In his office, he downloaded the software and took a picture of the photo of Virgil Caudill. He added twenty-five years, then long hair and a beard. He enlarged the photo, increased the contrast, and printed it. Johnny Boy left the office, got in the SUV, and headed east of town. If he was right, Virgil Caudill had two places he'd go.

On Old 60 he wound up behind a Chrysler that immediately cut its speed below the posted limit. He considered switching on the lights to make the car pull over so he could pass and make better time. It seemed like an unfair use of his position, which technically he was already engaged in. Looking into the Caudill man was more personal than professional.

Johnny Boy drove deep into the woods and began climbing the winding blacktop to a ridge, then turned into Bell Cemetery. A hundred years back it held graves of a single family, then four more married-ins. Over time the first family had died off or moved away, and other families started burying their dead here. Johnny Boy parked and reluctantly left his vehicle. During his high school years, it had been a place for teen-agers to drink, smoke, and brag. Johnny Boy had always made excuses to avoid such excursions and now he felt the familiar anxiety cut with paranoia. He'd never seen or heard a ghost, but believed they had specific powers, although he didn't know what those were. He opened the gate and stepped inside the cemetery. The markers were old and plain, unadorned except for the occasional small stone with an angel engraved on it, indicating an infant was buried there.

He began in the center at the oldest graves, studying the names, then expanded slowly outward. Caudill was the most com-mon name in the county and every cemetery held some. He could tell by proximity which bunch had married into this particular branch of Caudills. All the gravestones bore two dates, birth and death, separated by a hyphen. It struck him as immeasurably sad that an entire life was conveyed by a single small mark on a rock, a horizontal slash intended to convey thousands of days alive.

Near a copse of oak he found another row of Caudills, including the names he was hunting — Darly and Zale. Their old stones were thin and eroded along the top. Surrounding them were siblings and cousins, then kids, including their son Rupert and his wife Aline. Lying on top of Aline's grave was a freshly plucked black-eyed Susan.

Johnny Boy nodded to himself then swiftly left the cemetery.

Chapter Nineteen

On the six-hour drive to Rocksalt, Mick stopped for gasoline in Toledo and Cincinnati. Dusk fell like a veil, then full dark. He crossed the Ohio River into Newport, drove behind a hotel, and slept for an hour. Rested, he began the final leg home through a neighborhood known as Mansion Hill. He followed the river to Maysville, got on the double-lane AA Highway, and took the interstate into Rocksalt.

At the hospital, Mick found Raymond dozing in a chair beside Linda's bed. Mick entered the room without sound but Raymond snapped awake instantly, a marine on duty.

"How is she?" Mick said.

"Better," Raymond said. "Still doped up but stable. She's in and out. But when she's in, she's mainly mad and cusses like a sailor."

"That's a good sign."

"Where you been?"

"In a mess."

Raymond grunted and left. Mick sat in the chair he'd vacated, grateful for the warmth left in the upholstery. Linda's leg had been elevated, with a drainage tube running beneath the thick bandages. Three IV lines were taped to her arms. He squeezed Linda's hand, then settled into the chair and slept.

Nurses came and went in the night, then an orderly. Mick was awakened by his sister's voice complaining about the options for breakfast. A patient young man stood with a small piece of paper that passed for a menu.

"Cinnamon toast," Linda said.

"Not on here," the young man said. "Sorry."

They both looked at Mick as he stirred, his lower back aching from the chair and the driving. He suppressed a groan and stared at his sister.

"You hungry?" she said.

Mick nodded. She returned her attention to the young man.

"Bring one of everything on your damn list," she said. "Extra coffee."

"It's not hospital policy," he said.

"I'm the sheriff," Linda said. "Run get us

261

something to eat or I'll lock your ass up."

The young man scurried away. Mick grinned and Linda laughed briefly before cutting it short due to a spasm of pain. Mick went to the window and pulled open the curtain to a view of the parking lot. In the far corner sat his truck and he remembered what it contained and what he needed to do.

"I'm the deputy now," he said.

"I heard. Don't get used to it. You and Johnny Boy have any luck?"

"Some. I'll fill you in when it's done."

"You'll tell me now."

"First, I've got a few loose threads to take care of," Mick said. "Second, you ain't my boss. Johnny Boy is."

Suddenly exhausted, she shifted her head and aimed her vision at the ceiling.

"Damn it," she said. "Close those stupid curtains."

Mick complied and sat in the chair watching her sleep until the food arrived. He buttered hard slabs of toast for her, expecting resistance, surprised at her murmured gratitude. Linda inquired about the investigation and he stonewalled her again. This time she accepted it and dozed. A different doctor eventually entered the room. He referred to himself as "Dr. Bob" and spoke with the distinctive accent of Philadelphia. What he lacked in bedside manner, he made up for with humor and blunt answers. Linda faced at least six months of rehab. She'd make a full recovery, with the only long-term effect being a potentiality for arthritis.

"A potentiality," Linda said. "Is that even a word?"

"Yeah," Dr. Bob said. "Good enough for Aristotle, good enough for me. Any questions?"

"When can I get out of here?"

"Three days minimum. I'm still on the lookout for sepsis."

"On the lookout?" she said.

"My dad was a sailor in the merchant marine. I picked up his talk. He was superstitious, too. Scared of bananas. Supposed to be bad luck on a ship. I didn't eat one until I was twenty-five years old."

Linda grinned, laughed, and again stopped from pain.

"Don't laugh," Dr. Bob said. "It's not the best medicine."

"What is?"

"Rest. Do what your doctor says. Anything else?"

"Yeah," Mick said. "Can I bring food in for her?"

"Sure. Nobody should eat this crap."

263

He consulted his clipboard and glided out the door.

"Seems like a good doc," Mick said.

"Overpaid plumber."

"Uh-huh. You like him, don't you?"

"Hell, no. I don't like anybody."

"I'll get Raymond to bring you something to eat. You know his mom was here, right?"

"Shifty?"

"Yep, stayed the night. I got to go."

"Then go," Linda said. "You're already getting on my nerves."

Mick grinned and left. In the elevator he caught a whiff of himself and couldn't remember when he'd changed clothes. At least he'd slept and eaten. Long ago he'd locked onto a way of thinking based on observing a cement truck. The barrel rotated to prevent its load from solidifying while the truck simultaneously moved forward. He wondered what Aristotle would make of the potentialities.

Mick drove to the sheriff's office. The lot was empty except for a red hardtop convertible Miata. Mick parked beside it and entered the stone building through glass doors. Sandra sat behind her desk among the standard array of phones, a fax machine, a ten-year-old computer, and a manual typewriter. She was reading a library book.

"Your Miata? Is it new?" Mick said.

"No wonder you're the deputy."

"Uh, yeah."

He looked around the room to avoid her face. By local standards, she was a catch — early thirties, employed, divorced with no kids. Mick liked her for her intelligence and quick wit, the qualities many men preferred to ignore. But working together was an insurmountable obstacle to romance. Anyway, he'd be in Corsica soon.

"I need files on Hack Darvis and Pete Lowe," he said. "Any other pending cases?"

"Missing horse. Rumor of a fight at the high school. Eight bags of chips stolen from the Dollar General."

"Eight?"

"Yeah, a spree."

"Tell them we'll get to it."

Mick went into Johnny Boy's office, impressed as usual with its tidiness and order. A desk and chair, a utility table, and twenty-six filing cabinets. Centered on the desk were four files and a stack of index cards.

Two hours passed while Mick read the reports — first fast, then each one slowly. They were extremely detailed, including addresses, times, and full names of people. A full page was devoted to Pete's activities at the Bluestone Speedway. The gun that shot

Gowan was not recovered. Hack's Glock had recently fired a single bullet from its clip. Hack and Pete were killed by a twelve-gauge shotgun at close range. Both men lived alone and were involved with cock-fighting. According to an interview with Roscoe Reeder, the local fights had ended with Hack's death.

One file contained cell phone photos taken behind Hack's house — tire tracks and a shoe print with a 7 imprinted on the bottom and the name of the manufacturer. Two stores in town sold the brand, Iris. Other photographs depicted piles of sawdust and the smooth plane of logs cut by a chain-saw. He tucked the photographs in his pocket.

The last report was empty but had a heading: *Pete Lowe's daughter, Janice.* A hand-written note indicated that Linda had interviewed her the same day she'd gotten shot, so there was no record of their conversation. Johnny Boy hadn't gotten to a follow-up. Mick decided it was the best place to start.

Sandra was on the phone giving her best diplomatic mm-hmms, while making faces at Mick. She hung up and rolled her eyes.

"A woman heard an oddball noise in the woods. Her exact words, 'oddball noise.' I told her we'd send someone."

Mick nodded and left. He drove through Rocksalt, mostly empty except for new construction. A dentist's office had been torn down and replaced by a fast-food restaurant with metal outdoor tables bolted to a slab of cement. The hills were surrounded by trees that were being clear-cut and shipped away while the town was getting rebuilt in concrete and metal. He wondered where the construction material came from. Maybe they swapped timber for it.

Deep in the hills, he left the blacktop for a gravel road that gradually dissipated to dirt and ended at a yellow house built of wood. A four-wheel-drive vehicle was parked in the yard. A woman holding a hatchet stood in high weeds behind a large garden cart made of hard plastic. She wore a denim work jacket, old jeans, and green work boots that went nearly to her knees. She nodded to him, then left the weeds for a chopping block a few feet away. She placed a short log upright and swung the hatchet in a precise fashion, slicing a strip of wood that fell to the ground.

"I'm Jimmy Hardin's boy, Mick," he said. "Are you Mrs. Moore?"

"Not for a few years. I'm a Ms. now."

"I'm divorced myself," Mick said.

"If you're up here courting, I ain't in the market."

"No, ma'am. I understand. I was just making conversation."

"Why's that?"

"Well, the truth is, I'm trying to put you at ease. I'm a deputy. I came up here to ask about your father."

She took a step toward the garden cart and shifted her feet to a defensive stance, hefting the hatchet like a weapon.

"I talked to the sheriff a few days back. She's a woman. I'll thank you to get off my property."

Mick nodded and took a step backwards. He reached into his pocket and pulled out the badge.

"Ms. Lowe," he said. "You talked to Linda Hardin. She's my sister. She's in the hospital."

"She was okay when she left here."

"I know. Somebody shot her at Leo Gowan's house."

"I'm sorry to hear that. She struck me as nice. Warmhearted."

"Yes, she's that. She'll make it."

"Good," she said. "You here to tell me who killed Daddy?"

"No."

She turned to the chopping block and deftly cut off a two-inch-wide piece of kindling. Mick put the badge away and approached with his empty hands visible. He picked up the kindling and tossed it in the garden cart. She finished two more logs, then rested. Mick stepped into the high weeds and gripped the horizontal handle of the garden cart.

"Where to?" he said.

"I'll get it later. Thanks. Want some water?"

Mick nodded. With a flick of her wrist, she embedded the hatchet in the chopping block and turned away. He followed her onto the porch. She removed her boots, set them beside a small pair of canvas sneakers, and entered the house. Janice returned wearing leather slippers, carrying two tall glasses of water with ice.

"Sit anywhere," she said, and eased into a wooden chair with a red cushion tied onto the seat. Mick dragged a chair farther away and turned it to face her.

"Thanks," he said, and sat.

An aura of loneliness surrounded Janice, not the sort that came from pushing people away, but from avoiding them.

"Your dad," he said. "He have any problems with folks?"

"No, I told your sister that. All he did was work on cars. Did you talk to them?"

"The other deputy did. According to his notes, people said your dad was the best mechanic around. Stubborn and independent. Wouldn't work for just anybody, not even for more money."

"Sounds like Daddy."

"Did you know he asked Roscoe Reeder to keep a chicken for him?"

"Why would he do that?"

"According to Roscoe, it's a fighting cock. Supposed to be worth a lot of money. Somebody threatened him over it."

"How much money?" she said quickly, then looked at the yard.

"Three grand," Mick said.

"Want more water?"

Mick nodded. She rose swiftly and carried the glasses inside. Mick considered their brief conversation. Most people would want to know who had threatened their father, not how much the rooster was worth. She'd changed the subject immediately. He glanced at the screen door. The rubber work boots appeared much broader than the canvas shoes and he wondered if she wore two pair of socks. The boots were probably lined. He stood and moved silently to the door, squatted and turned over one of the sneakers. The sole bore the number 7 along with the name of its maker — Iris. Through the screen door he could hear water running from a faucet. He quickly pulled out Johnny Boy's photographs and compared the footprint to the sole of the sneaker by the door. They matched.

He returned to his chair and faced the sloping yard. A breeze blew a terrible scent. Janice stepped outside with the water. She wrinkled her nose at the smell.

"I keep a few hogs," she said. "They're downwind, but sometimes a gust comes this way."

"When I was a boy I used to help a man get food for his hogs. We went to all the grade schools in the county and picked up garbage cans filled with the lunch slop. Then we'd go to his house and feed the hogs."

"Smart," she said. "Free food."

"That's exactly what he said. He drank a lot and I quit. I mean a lot. Whiskey all day every day. All his kids left as soon as they could. Reason I got the job was his youngest boy took off. Had a wandering eye."

"Was he married?"

"No. I mean one eye drifted off to the side. He looked at everything with his head cocked. Supposed to make him real good at shooting pool. His daddy, though, he fell off

271

the back of his pickup truck head first into one of those garbage cans full of slop. Drowned in it."

"Looks like it would tip over with him in it."

"He was real short. Should've mentioned that."

"Where's all this coming from?" she said.

"The smell of your hogs made me think of it."

He gestured to the garden cart.

"You cut your own wood?" he said.

"Yeah, keeps me fit."

"I used to quarter logs with an axe for my grandfather. All I ever wanted was one of those automatic splitters."

"My cousin had one," she said. "He lost three fingers to it."

"Chainsaw's safer than people know."

"I use the battery kind."

"How long's a battery last?"

"Forty volt will run me about two hours. Three on small stuff."

"What size bar?"

"Fourteen inch," she said. "Is this like the slop story? Some short drunk going to fall on a chainsaw?"

A bobolink called its bubbling song. Mick watched it fly to the ground and enter a patch of high weeds at the edge of the

272

woods. Its flat head was bisected vertically by color, which meant it was a male. Mick knew there was a nest in there.

"Thing is," he said, "every chainsaw's got a unique pattern. The marks it leaves on wood. It's like DNA. What do you think I'd find if I compared your chainsaw to the marks on that tree behind Hack Darvis's place? The knocked-down tree somebody cut up to get a car through? Think the pattern is the same as your chainsaw?"

"What do I think? That's what you're asking me?"

Mick nodded.

"What I think is," she said, "you're full of shit."

"You're right," he said. "I made all that up."

"Why would you do that?"

"Because those shoes by the door are the same as the footprints where Hack Darvis got killed. Iris size seven."

She glanced at the shoes then held Mick's gaze. Wind blew from the other direction, bringing with it the scent of Queen Anne's lace, the loamy smell of carrots. Two squirrels squabbled in the grass. One ran up the tree and continued out of sight into the high boughs. A startled cardinal flew to a bush.

"May as well tell me everything," Mick said.

"I don't need another man trying to fix me."

"I'm not him," Mick said. "I'm a guy sitting in the sun willing to listen. I can't tell you how many after-action reviews I went through. Not a one did me any good. Just paper turned in to please the desk jockeys. A way for the brass to justify bad decisions, mostly. But talking to another soldier who'd been in the same boat. That got me through."

"Combat?"

"Hundred and First Airborne. You?"

"Two tours as a medic. Third Infantry Brigade Combat Team, Twenty-Fifth Division. My job was to keep soldiers healthy outside the wire. Now I do the same with hogs."

"Did your dad know Hack?"

"Yeah, since they were kids. Daddy got into chickens after my mom died. Just laying hens. Then them damn fighting birds. He knew cars but not roosters. He put the last of his money into buying a rooster. Charles, he called it. Said the car owners were the big winners, not the drivers. And Charles was the best car on the track. He loved that bird."

"I heard he was a good man."

"He was. But didn't have much understanding of the way things work. Really work. Especially Hack and those bird fights."

"What do you mean?" Mick said.

"Hack fixed the fights and made money off them."

"How?"

"Gambling. Hack paired the birds. What he did was put a strong bird against a weak one. Everybody knew the strong bird would win. They'd give odds on the weak bird. Hack smeared snake venom on the gaffs of the weak birds, then bet against the favorites. One little cut and the favorite died. Hack cleaned up."

"He couldn't have done all that himself."

"No, he had two guys from Vanceburg in on it. Daddy said they made gobs of money. Then they quit coming and Hack, he wanted Daddy to go in with him and poison Charles. But Daddy didn't like cheating. And he didn't want Charles to die that way. Not even for half the money."

"How do you know all this?"

"Daddy told me. He came here and asked me to keep Charles for him. I didn't have a coop. I told him to bring it back in a few days and I'd cobble something together. He said he couldn't wait a few days. Said Hack threatened to kill Charles if Daddy didn't cheat with him. Mostly I set here and think, if I'd took that damn bird, Daddy would still be alive."

"Everybody thinks that way when somebody dies."

"Sometimes it's true."

Mick nodded, thinking of his own regrets about the deaths of comrades. He hadn't been responsible but had felt that way. It was natural, something to avoid.

"Then what?" Mick said.

"After I found Daddy, I knew Hack killed him."

"Did you tell anybody?"

"Nobody to tell," she said. "What I did was start watching Hack. He drove a four-wheeler around. Carried two guns. A Glock on his hip. And a shotgun strapped to the roll bar. I figured it was the same shotgun he killed Daddy with. So I waited till he left the ATV. I took the shotgun in case the law needed proof. He saw me."

"Did he say anything?"

"Yeah. Said he killed Daddy and wasn't afraid of a girl. He'd fuck me so hard it'd pack the ground down."

Mick nodded, knowing he needed to tread carefully.

"Then what happened?" he said.

"He shot the Glock. Missed me."

Mick continued to nod, thinking about Johnny Boy's file that said one bullet was missing from the clip. He could guess Janice's response to being shot at, the instinct of a soldier. He waited for more but she remained silent, staring at him with her calm gaze. He spoke in a gentle, conversational tone.

"After he shot," Mick said, "what'd you do?"

"I came home."

Mick thought it through. Her story answered a lot of questions right down to the rattlesnake in Hack's shed. He knew she'd used the shotgun on Hack Darvis. He also knew she'd never admit it. The only evidence was the shoes, circumstantial at best. They were available in town, which meant plenty of people owned a pair. It would be impossible to prove she had made the footprints in the photographs.

A breeze carried the scent of honeysuckle. The clouds drifted and light slipped through the treetops as if through gauze. If she confessed, he'd have to take her into custody.

"What would you do," she said, "if somebody killed your father?"

"My dad drank himself to death when I was little."

"Well, my daddy didn't have the chance to."

She nodded, folded her hands in her lap, tipped her head back, and closed her eyes. Mick watched her intently. He'd experienced PTSD and seen many forms of it but she didn't display any standard signs. Maybe she was good at hiding them. He doubted it though. Concealing emotion took practice and she was clearly someone who was rarely around people.

"Where's the shotgun?" he said.

"Under the garden cart."

He wondered if it was a trick, a booby trap she'd learned in the desert, a live grenade propped beneath the axle.

"Why would you keep it there?" he said.

"I don't. I carry it with me in case somebody from Hack's family shows up. Heard your truck and hid the shotgun."

"How'd you know I wasn't a Darvis?"

"You look like your sister."

Mick stood, went to the garden cart, and circled it slowly, looking for a tripwire. He tipped the cart backward. Nestled in the weeds was a Savage double-barrel shotgun. He picked it up and checked the breech. It was loaded. He kept the action open, propped in the crook of his elbow. She sat on the porch watching him. She hadn't moved and he understood that she was waiting for him to arrest her.

"I checked into Hack Darvis," he said. "He's got no kids. Rest of his family moved away."

She nodded once.

"I need those shoes," he said.

She picked up the faded canvas sneakers and carried them across the yard. She offered them to him. He didn't move and she tossed them in the cart. Still holding the shotgun, he retrieved the shoes and walked toward his truck.

"Hey," she said.

He stopped and turned around, wondering if she held a small pistol. The thought came and went during his pivoting motion before he faced her. She was a soldier. If she'd wanted him dead, she wouldn't have called to him first. She held a piece of kindling.

"What are you going to do?" she said.

"I don't know yet."

He put the shotgun and shoes in his truck and climbed behind the wheel. She hadn't moved. He rolled the window down and spoke.

"If you get mixed up in anything else, I'll

lock you up so fast it'll make your head spin."

He drove to the blacktop and stopped on the shoulder, wondering if he was making a mistake. First Penny, now Janice. He hoped he wasn't letting them go because they were women. No, he'd arrested his share of female soldiers. He'd had to fight two, one of whom stabbed him. Maybe it was civilian life, the blurred lines, the lack of strict protocols. He'd never questioned himself before. Since retirement he did it every day. He put the truck in gear and eased back onto the road.

If someone had killed his grandfather, he'd have done the same as her. He'd killed men in anger, but that didn't necessarily mean he'd do it again. He didn't believe she would either. Maybe he didn't want to arrest people for things he'd do himself. His grandfather would say Mick was following the code of the hills. Mick hoped it was true.

CHAPTER TWENTY

Joe Tiller had lost everything he'd ever cared about — brother murdered, wife dead of cancer, one son killed in the Gulf War, the other boy stabbed to death in prison. In his own way, Joe had lost himself by changing his name and living half his life in Montana and Alaska. Now that he was back in Eldridge County, he hoped nobody knew him. How could they? He had a pot belly, gray hair, and a long beard. His once well-muscled arms had transformed to stringy limbs. He was sixty, looked seventy, and felt a hundred.

He'd driven nearly five thousand miles, sleeping in his car or at cheap motels. He wished he were a machine that he could take to a shop and get serviced — dismantled, oiled, and reassembled with a few new parts. The long journey had been hard on his bad leg. A kid had shot him more than twenty-five years ago. The bullet had lodged against his bone and Joe had foolishly tried to shoot it out with a pistol. A big mistake, not the first and not the worst. Killing a man was the worst and Joe was beginning to think that coming back home was next worst.

He barely recognized Rocksalt, only a few buildings on Main Street — the old ten-cent store, a church, the courthouse. Railroad Street was gone. Maloney's was gone. Half the town purported to be antique stores selling items from the 1990s: vinyl records, action figures, and time-saving devices purchased via television. One thing he'd learned — time was never saved, it was either curtailed or stretched longer than necessary. If time could genuinely be saved, rich folks would have bought it all up a long time ago.

The hospital had swallowed one end of town while the college had overtaken the other end. Eventually they'd meet in the middle and engage in real-estate combat. He felt a pang of relief when he saw a familiar store — Whitley's Grocery — still situated on the town line. It seemed smaller than he remembered. The interior layout was the same with six aisles of staple goods and a single cash register up front. A young woman with multiple earrings and a full sleeve tattoo used a portable device to scan the prices of his purchases. He asked if she was a Whitley and she hadn't understood the question. He paid cash, as he had for decades, leaving no electronic trail.

Joe carried two plastic bags of food to his car. Out of habit he checked the tires and the oil. Satisfied, he got in his car and headed east into the wooded hills. After a few miles he relaxed. The contour of the land was familiar and offered some comfort. Two hard curves had been straightened, which was the first good change he'd seen. He recalled a triple S-curve that had caused multiple wrecks, including a school bus he'd been riding to high school. At the time, the accident had been the most exciting event in his life. He wished it still was.

He'd been staying at the old home place since his return, having found it like a migrating bird returning to its old nest. The house was barely standing. The porch posts had rotted away and the roof had fallen forward like a trapdoor. The interior had been a mess of beer cans and cigarette butts. A broken bong lay in a corner. His childhood home had become a party house for kids.

He'd cleaned it, recalling the exact placement of furniture — the couch beneath a window, his mother's chair, a large rug that had belonged to his grandmother. An old hand at camping, Joe had inflated an air mattress and slept in the most sheltered corner of the front room. He ate from cans heated over a sterno stove and performed basic repairs. The house was a receptacle of memory but the best memory was from Montana — entering a natural hot spring with Botree twenty-five years ago. They stayed together until she died. A year later he loaded the Wagoneer and came home, having missed Kentucky every day.

Now he stopped at the foot of his family hill, shifted into four-wheel drive, and drove on. It was his fourth Wagoneer, an ideal vehicle for the mountains of Montana and the snowy terrain of Alaska. His parents and brother were dead and he hadn't spoken to his sister in decades. He supposed his nephews were grown and he hoped they'd fared better than his own boys.

The road petered out completely and he kept going, veering around saplings and full-grown trees. He parked, gathered his groceries, and entered the house. A young man stood inside wearing the uniform of law enforcement with a holstered sidearm. Joe nodded to him and set his provisions on a makeshift table made of scrap lumber laid over two buckets. He moved to the only chair, repaired with wire and duct tape. He stared at the cop and waited.

"I'm the sheriff of Eldridge County," the man said. "Who are you?"

"Joe Tiller."

"What are you doing here?"

"Just passing through. I apologize if it's your land. I don't think I hurt anything. Tried to fix it up a little."

"Why'd you do that if you're passing through?"

"My way, I guess. Even when I rented, I always worked on the place."

The sheriff gestured to a toolbox in the corner.

"You travel with tools?" he said.

"A few basics," Joe said. "Old habit. I'm headed to Florida."

"Where you from?"

"Here and there. Mostly north."

"I seen your vehicle in town. No license plate."

"It's in the back seat. The little struts rusted over. I ain't got around to drilling them out yet. I can show you the plate if you want."

"No, you stay right there," the sheriff said. "Got any ID?"

"Yup."

285

"Toss your wallet over here. Easy."

Joe hauled the worn leather billfold from his pocket. He threw it underhanded at the sheriff's boots, where it raised a tiny cloud of dust on impact. The sheriff picked it up, withdrew the driver's license, and tipped it to catch light. He studied it, then looked at Joe.

"Alaska. You're a long way from home, Mr. Tiller."

"Winters started getting to me."

"I heard it got so cold that car tires turned square overnight."

"I never saw that," Joe said. "But it got sixty below for a month one year."

"Most men carry more in their wallet."

"I don't need much."

"No credit cards. No emergency contact. No family pictures."

"I'm a little low on all that right now."

"You know whose house this is?"

"Can't say as I do."

"It was Darly and Zale Caudill's place. Then their boy and his wife, Rupert and Aline."

Joe gathered a deep breath at the mention of his parents. He released the air slowly, then breathed deeply again. He'd been in worse spots but not for a long time. The sheriff was too young to know about Joe's

286

trouble in Eldridge County. Somebody must have seen his car and called the law. It was the way of the hills — neighbors looking out for each other even if they lived miles away. Probably an older woman living alone. A man would've come up here himself.

The sheriff glanced up from the driver's license.

"Chicken," the sheriff said. "Is that really the name of your town up there?"

"Yep."

"Funny name."

"What I heard, they wanted to call it Ptarmigan because a lot of those birds live up there. The old timers couldn't figure out how to spell it so they picked Chicken."

"Where's it at, 'Chicken'?"

"Interior. Southeast of Fairbanks."

"Near Canada?"

Joe nodded. He didn't care for the conversation but needed to be cooperative, or appear so anyhow.

"I like maps," the sheriff said. "Got a big collection of them. They's some to say they're outdated now, irrelevant on account of the internet. Why do you need a paper map when you got a phone? But me, I don't see things that way. One day we'll need those paper maps again. I collect them and

I study them. If I remember right, Fairbanks ain't too far from Canada. That right?"

"I'd say five or six hour drive. In the summer. Roads are closed in winter."

"And where's Chicken located? In relation to Fairbanks, I mean?"

"About five hours southeast."

The sheriff stared at him for a long time, then looked at the driver's license again. A patient man by nature, Joe had further developed the skill by enduring the long winters of Alaska. He sat without moving, hearing his own breath. A fly entered through a broken window, circled in reconnaissance, and landed on the table by the groceries. From outside came the in-flight call of a pileated woodpecker. It had been Joe's favorite bird. He used to know their lifespan but the information had slipped away and he wondered how much else he'd lost. Enough to walk in on a lawman.

"Here's what I think," the sheriff said. "I think you picked Chicken because it's close to Canada in case you had to run. I think 'Joe Tiller' is an alias. I think you're Virgil Caudill. I think you came to this house because you grew up in it. I think you killed my cousin. Billy Rodale."

"What makes you think I'm that Caudill man?"

"Eyes and eyebrows. Cheekbones. You can grow all the beard you want, but the eyes and brow ridge don't change."

Joe thought about this. Botree had long ago suggested he pluck a new pattern into his eyebrows but he resisted. They'd been safe in Chicken. After her death, there was nothing to stay for. Joe took a deep breath, then two more, letting them out slow and easy. He was tired and sore, sitting in his mother's house. The time had come.

"I'm Virgil Caudill," he said.

His entire body relaxed — every limb, muscle, and tendon. He felt a cellular relief at speaking his own name after twenty-five years. Maybe that's why he'd returned.

"Is this still yet Caudill land?" he said.

"According to the courthouse, yeah. Ain't been sold. Your sister pays the taxes on it."

"Where's she at?"

"Dayton, Ohio. Her husband got a job up there."

"Marlon," Virgil said. "He could fix anything. What about Abigail Trent?"

"I know a bunch of Trents, but not her."

"She'd be about my age. Probably got married and changed her name. She was my fiancée back then. Or everybody thought so. I don't know what we were exactly."

"You got a gun on you?" Johnny Boy said.

"Yeah. A pistol."

"How about you take it out slow and set it down."

"No, I ain't ready to do that yet."

Johnny Boy adjusted his position and unsnapped the strap on his holster.

"How'd you find me?" Virgil said.

"I saw you three times. Once getting gas in Fleming County. Twice in town. Checked the motel and campgrounds. Figured the only other place was the cemetery or here. I saw a fresh black-eyed Susan on your mother's grave."

"It was her favorite. That and a sunflower. She planted them together. Said they were the same family, little and big."

"Why'd you come back?" Johnny Boy said.

"I been asking myself that since I walked in. You going to arrest me or kill me?"

"I been asking myself that, too."

The two men looked each other hard in the eyes. Both were seeing a version of themselves — past and future. Neither liked it.

"I want to know everything," Johnny Boy said. "From the top down to now."

Virgil nodded. His impulse was to take a minute to assemble it all in his mind, but he realized he didn't need to. He'd been waiting for years to tell it. He didn't expect the listener to be a kid-sheriff in Kentucky, let alone a cousin to Rodale.

"How long you been sheriff?" Virgil said.

"A few days. Why?"

"You look young for it."

"It's temporary. Now get on with it."

"My brother Boyd was plumb wild back then. Drank and gambled, chased women and wrecked cars. Boyd got killed and everybody knew Rodale did it. I mean everybody — my family, the whole hill, half the county. The sheriff, too. He come to the house and said he'd look the other way if something happened to Rodale."

"Was that Troy Johnson?" Johnny Boy said.

"Yep, ol' Troy."

"Why would he say that?"

"Used to date my sister is why. You got any more questions or you want me to tell it?"

"I won't say nothing till you're done."

"I worked on the garbage truck for the college in town. A four-man crew. They all knew about Boyd. Abigail, too. And every single man, woman, and child was on me to do something about it. But I never. I ain't built that way. Boyd, he was. If it'd been me dead, he'd have killed Rodale the next day. I thought if I waited long enough, it'd go away, but nothing does in these hills. What I did was get a birth certificate in the name of Joe Tiller. Found the name in a cemetery, a kid born the same year as me, but died young. I used the birth certificate to get a new social security number and driver's license. It was easier to do that stuff in the nineties. I bought a car and registered it to Joe Tiller. I left it at the airport in Cincinnati and came back home."

He stopped, slightly out of breath. He'd been talking faster than usual because it was the first time he didn't have to be careful and not give himself away. In Alaska he rarely talked to anyone, never anything personal, and always carefully measured. He took a breath and began again.

"I watched Rodale's house for a week. He never left. Scared to go out, I reckon. He'd heard all the same talk as me. What I did was use a lawnmower muffler to make a silencer for my pistol. Then I walked in his house and shot him six times. Drove to the Cincinnati airport. Left my car there so people would think I'd flown somewhere. Then got in the car I'd bought and drove it to Missoula, Montana. Up there I rented a cabin on Rock Creek. Met a woman and moved with her to Alaska. She had two boys from two men before me. We lived outside of Fairbanks for a few years. It was growing fast and we moved to Chicken. Been there ever since. My wife died and I came home."

He quit talking long enough for Johnny Boy to understand that he was finished. Virgil seemed both tired and invigorated simultaneously. Johnny Boy understood the pressure Virgil had been under to avenge his brother. Johnny Boy had been taught a similar anger toward Virgil's branch of the Caudill family.

"Twenty-five years living up there," Johnny Boy said. "What'd you do all that time?"

"Hunted. Fished. Cut timber, split it, and stacked it. Read a lot."

"How'd you get books?"

"Library. In Alaska they'll mail them to you."

"Get anything out of them?"

"Yeah. Humans are the only animal that kills in reprisal. Been doing it since the beginning of time. What that means is, we're all descended from revenge killers. It's in us deep. We're a vengeful bunch."

"Not all of us."

Virgil shifted as if his lower back was bothering him from the spindly wooden chair.

"You are, too," Virgil said. "It's why you're here."

"No. I'm here to arrest you for murder."

CHAPTER TWENTY-ONE

Mick was nearly back to town when his phone chirped to indicate a message. He usually had it off and tucked away but he'd kept it handy since Linda was hospitalized. The sound gave him a jolt of fear that she'd taken a turn for the worse. He pulled over to read a text from Johnny Boy.

SOS. Old Caudill place. Now.

Mick turned around and drove back the way he'd come. He knew the location from a couple of years ago. Dusk was transforming the hills into dark humps on both sides of the road, and a few early stars speckled the sky like a light frost on hard grass. He headed east, turned onto a narrow blacktop road, and found the remnants of a dirt road. The ground was too rough for rear-wheel drive. He parked and climbed the hill with his flashlight and gun. He saw the dark roof of the house first, then the Jeep Wagoneer parked in front. He entered the woods and circled the house, finding the sheriff's big SUV parked in back. Around front was a man sitting on the broken steps. Mick raised his Beretta. Standing in the heavy shadow of an oak, he spoke.

"Don't move," Mick said. "Put your hands in front of you."

"It's me," Johnny Boy said.

Mick stepped into the dim moonlight.

"You all right?" he said.

"Not really," Johnny Boy said.

He gestured behind him. Mick stepped onto the porch and entered the house. A man lay on the floor beside a chair, a gun near his hand, blood pooled beneath him. Mick pressed two fingers to his carotid artery. He went back outside. Johnny Boy still sat facing the woods.

"Anybody else here?" Mick said.

"No."

"You find him like this?"

Johnny Boy shook his head slowly.

A shred of cloud drifted from its place in front of the moon. The light intensified. Mick kept his eyes moving, letting his peripheral vision hold Johnny Boy in sight. Even in the stark shadows of night, he looked bad, as if recovering from a long illness. Mick pitched his voice low and soothing.

"Who was he, Johnny Boy?"

"Virgil Caudill. I came up here to arrest him."

"Did he resist?"

"Maybe. Something."

"How did it go?"

"He pulled a gun. I went for mine. He never shot. He could've. He turned his chest toward me like he was wanting to give me a better target. Smiling a little. I shot him twice. I didn't have to."

"He had a gun in his hand," Mick said.

"He wasn't going to shoot. I knew it but I killed him anyhow. I wish I hadn't."

"That's good," Mick said. "You're supposed to wish that. If you didn't, there'd be something wrong with you."

Johnny Boy set his gun and badge on the steps beside him.

"You're the sheriff now," he said. "I quit. You need to arrest me."

"No."

"I killed him."

Mick tucked his Beretta away and sat beside Johnny Boy.

"You shot a suspect with a gun," Mick said.

"You got to take me in."

"In Eldridge County, everybody knows you, right? You can talk to anybody anytime about damn near anything. You're an unlikely lawman. That's what makes you so good at it. You hearing me?"

Johnny Boy shrugged then nodded.

"You go to prison," Mick said, "and all that's done with. You're nothing but a locked-up cop. Every man in there hates cops. They will rape you, then kill you."

Johnny Boy's misery rippled off him in waves, the ebb and flow of guilt and sorrow. Mick had experienced it many times. There was no cure. He had tried them all — whiskey, sex, solitude, gambling, and drugs. Either you figured out a way to accept things or they would destroy you. Johnny Boy was poised to go either way.

"That Caudill man," Mick said. "What was he wanted for?"

"Homicide. He sat in the chair and admitted it."

"Way I see it," Mick said, "you got three options. You can run. You can go to jail. Or you can tell the State Police what happened. There'll be an investigation but you'll be cleared."

"You sure about that?"

"You shot a fugitive who pulled a gun on you."

"In his family home."

"This place?" Mick said.

"He grew up here. I killed him on his own land. I don't want everybody knowing that about me."

An inkling of a solution surfaced in the back of Mick's mind then retreated, leaving just enough behind for him to examine. He circled it in his mind. The idea was like an iceberg with only 10 percent visible. Another thought protruded, then another.

A barred owl gave its long call — who cooks for you, who cooks for you all? Then a gurgle, as if a Spaniard were rolling his *r*'s underwater. It was a territorial call and Mick waited for another owl, farther away, to answer. Instead of fighting, owls declared their presence then respected one another's space. They saved their killing for prey, which never got away.

"Got a passport?" Mick said.

"Yeah. Never used it. Me and my last girlfriend were supposed to go to Mexico. We broke up. Cost me a hundred and ten bucks. Waste of money. Now, I've wasted everything. My whole damn life."

The moon had risen nearly overhead, reflecting light across the land and glinting on the Wagoneer. Mick's idea was simple. The main obstacle was Johnny Boy, his guilt and sense of responsibility.

"I got a friend from a mining town in Wales," Mick said. "Sebastien was in SAS, British Special Forces, then he joined the French Foreign Legion. If you're in the Legion and you get wounded, you automatically qualify as a French citizen. That happened to him and he moved to Corsica. Know where that is?"

"Island in the Mediterranean."

"I'm supposed to be there now but I couldn't go because of Linda. I rented a two-room place from him, paid in advance for six months. You can go there."

"I ain't running."

"You can trust Sebastien. When you need to, you can talk to him. If you don't want to talk, you don't have to. Sebastien hardly ever says a word. I'll take care of things here."

"What things?"

"The whole mess. I'll keep you out of it. When you're ready, come back home. I mean really ready. Not just homesick, but ready to be a deputy again. Linda'll recover and she'll need you."

"If I run off, everybody'll know I killed Caudill. That takes away my reason for leaving."

"I'll say I did it."

"Why?"

"You're in a jam," Mick said, "and I can help you."

"That's it?"

"That's all things ever are. If you don't help when you can, there might not be anybody to help you when you need it."

Johnny Boy stared into the darkness of the treeline. A brief wind rubbed leaves against each other, the sound as soft as velvet. A cicada gave a tentative squeak as if signaling safety to its brethren. The air filled with their sound, rising and falling like distant surf.

Johnny Boy heaved a long, hard sigh.

"All right," he said.

Mick went in the house and retrieved the dead man's pistol. Outside, Johnny Boy handed him his badge and gun.

"Your gun," Mick said. "Is it county issue or your own?"

"Mine."

"Good. Are you okay to drive?"

Johnny Boy nodded.

"Follow me to your place."

They drove slowly to town in a convoy of two. Mick was surprised at the Spartan décor of Johnny Boy's apartment — no couch, no coffee table, and one chair, a recliner with a lamp angled to shine over his left shoulder. Floor-to-ceiling book-shelves lined the walls, organized by subject and alphabetized by author. Most surprising was the presence of a yoga mat unrolled on the floor.

While Johnny Boy showered and packed, Mick booked him a flight to Bastia Poretta Airport in Corsica. He sent a coded text to an international number that would eventually find its way to Sebastien. He deleted the SOS text from Johnny Boy. Twenty minutes later, Johnny Boy carried a suitcase into the living room. Mick had never seen him in civilian clothes before — the standard blue jeans, boots, and work shirt of the hills.

"I'm not sure about this," Johnny Boy said.

"Second thoughts are a good sign. Means you're turning things over in your head, not just reacting. That's what you were doing at the Caudill house. You were ready to go to prison. Now it's France instead."

"Does this go away?"

"How you feel? No. It stays. Gets easier to deal with but it'll always be with you. If not, you're a psychopath. We need to leave. Got your passport?"

"Yeah."

Mick withdrew his wallet and pulled out

four hundred dollars.

"Take this. Don't use a credit card. If you run out of money, Sebastien will lend you some. We'll square everything up when you come home."

"What about my ticket?"

"I paid for it. You can pay me back later. Right now, you need to write a letter to Sandra and Linda. A letter, not an email. You're taking temporary leave for a family thing."

"Like what?"

"Medical is best. Nobody questions it. Where's the farthest away you got a cousin?"

"Muncie, Indiana."

"That'll work."

"Anything else?"

"Yes. Call my cell phone. I'll answer. After thirty seconds hang up."

Johnny Boy nodded and made the call. Mick answered and they stared at each other silently, both mentally counting the seconds. Johnny Boy ended the call.

"Now what?" Johnny Boy said.

"Leave your phone here. If you use it, it'll put you in Corsica and the whole thing comes apart. Now write your letter."

"Damn, you think of everything, don't you?"

"Yeah," Mick said. "I should've been a criminal."

"Like Virgil Caudill? Like me?"

"Did he plan out killing your cousin?"

"Said he did. Made a silencer from a lawnmower muffler."

"That's the difference, Johnny Boy. You didn't plan it. You went there to arrest him and he pulled a gun on you. Now go write that letter."

The drive to Blue Grass Airport in Lexington took more than two hours, with Mick staying five miles under the speed limit. A routine stop by police would reveal his ready bag still full of combat supplies, three guns used in murders, and Caudill's pistol. Johnny Boy sat nearly immobile, staring out the side window, occasionally grunting to himself, and shaking his head.

"Your car," Mick said. "If you went to Muncie, it'd be gone. Give me the keys."

Johnny Boy dug in his pocket for a ring of four metal keys attached to a shredded rabbit's foot, bones protruding through scraps of fur.

"Car. Apartment. Two for work."

"How long you had this rabbit foot?"

"My grandfather gave it to me on my twelfth birthday. I wanted a pocketknife. But he said I needed luck more."

They passed through the starless night. The hills gradually lowered themselves to the rolling land of Fayette County with its white fences flashing in the headlights. Mick rolled his window down an inch to direct wind on his face and keep him alert. He took the exit for New Circle Road that circumvented Lexington, got on Man O' War Boulevard, and turned onto the airport's entrance of Terminal Drive. He parked at departures. Johnny Boy didn't move.

"I don't like running away," Johnny Boy said.

"You're not, you're being smart."

"Are you?"

"I don't know," Mick said. "I got to get back and check on Linda."

Johnny Boy left the truck and removed his luggage from the bed. He walked around the cab to Mick's window.

"Thanks, Mick," Johnny Boy said.

Mick nodded, watching Johnny Boy walk into a future he couldn't comprehend. Aside from the language, island life was similar to Eldridge County, bounded by sea instead of hills. Mick felt a twinge of envy that he wasn't leaving.

He put the truck in gear and drove. The airport was next to Keeneland Race Course.

Thoroughbreds had veterinarians on perpetual call, the finest food available, and air-conditioned stalls. It occurred to Mick that a horse in Lexington had a better life than Johnny Boy would in Corsica.

CHAPTER TWENTY-TWO

Mick drove through Rocksalt and left the county, following a winding road beneath an interwoven canopy of tree limbs to Sand Plank Pay Lake. He removed Virgil Caudill's pistol from the duffel bag, walked to the edge of the water, and hurled it into the lake. The splash was small. Within seconds the placid surface appeared the same as before, flat from the moonlight. He'd disposed of guns here two years ago and figured one more wouldn't matter. What's another bone to a stew?

He drove back into Eldridge County and turned onto the overgrown lane to the Caudill house. There were no new tracks. Inside, the dead man lay undisturbed. Flies had already found him. Mick waved them away, a useless effort. He returned to his truck and put the Beretta in the glove box. He wiped Johnny Boy's pistol thoroughly, then passed it from hand to hand several times.

He pulled the slide twice, making sure there were enough prints to appear as if he'd been handling it for a while. He fired one shot into the woods and put the gun into his back pocket.

That left Gowan's gun, the big .45 revolver he'd gotten from Penny in Detroit. He wiped it down very carefully, then unloaded the four rounds, and cleaned each bullet before reinserting them into the cylinder. Using an old T-shirt from under the passenger seat, he wiped Hack Darvis's shotgun, paying special attention to the bore. He wanted to remove any latent fingerprints left by Janice Lowe as well as his own.

In the house, he squatted beside the corpse and wrapped the stiffening left hand around the fore end of the shotgun. He squeezed the man's right hand against the grip and trigger, then carefully leaned the shotgun against a wall. Next he inserted Caudill's right forefinger into the trigger guard of Gowan's big .45. Turning his head, Mick fired the gun into the wall. The sound reverberated in the small space. Mick dropped the dead man's hand to the floor. The whole undertaking was crude, he knew, and wouldn't stand up to careful scrutiny, but there wouldn't be much. The evidence would speak for itself.

The only hitch to his plan was rigor mortis and time of death. Marquis might send the body to Lexington for a full forensic examination. But Mick figured solving three murders and the attempted murder of a law enforcement official would hurry things along. Especially if Chief Logan made the logical conclusion that Mick had arranged.

He figured he had fifteen hours before Johnny Boy's letter was delivered to the sheriff's office. He went to his truck and set an alarm on his phone for seven hours, then slept. When he awoke it was full day. He made a series of calls — Rocksalt Police, an ambulance, then Sandra at dispatch. He sat on the steps with Johnny Boy's pistol on his lap, relaxing while he could.

Ten hours later he sat in the Rocksalt police station with Chief Logan and Lieutenant Fred Sanders from the State Police Critical Response Team. Sanders was assisting due to his experience with officer-involved shootings. He was tall and thin with broad shoulders that looked grafted onto his body from another man. After eight years in the navy, Sanders had joined the state police, moving rapidly up the ranks from trooper to lieutenant. As a former sailor he was predisposed against Mick and had been making it clear for hours. Mick wondered if it was more personal than the standard army-navy rivalry.

They sat around a table that had computer jacks in the center and a push-button console for audio recording. Mick wore a T-shirt that was too big, having handed over his own shirt to test for gunshot residue. He'd also turned in Johnny Boy's gun and claimed it as his own. After waiving his rights to an attorney, he'd told the same story a dozen times. Mick had interrogated enough suspects to know what to do — and more importantly what not to do, such as use the exact phrasing each time as if from memorization. He deliberately made slight shifts in sequence and detail. Sanders had picked at everything. If Mick were in his position, he'd do the same because the whole thing stunk.

The interview was winding down but Mick still needed two more items covered and he had to wait until someone else brought them up. He was prolonging the conversation to give them time to do so. There was a knock at the door and Officer Dixon entered. He motioned to Chief Logan, who left the room. Lieutenant Sanders switched off the recording device.

"Looks good so far," he said. "Righteous."

Mick nodded. During interrogations for

the CID he'd turned off the main tape and left an auxiliary running. The trick had enabled him to gain crucial evidence that put away two killers.

"Need anything?" Sanders said. "Smoke or bathroom?"

Mick shook his head.

"Want to call anybody?"

Mick frowned as if thinking it over. The man had inadvertently stumbled into one of the subjects that Mick wanted to cover, but with Logan gone and the recorder turned off, he was hesitant. The door opened and Logan returned. Lieutenant Sanders flicked on the recording switch. When the machine began its hum, Logan started talking.

"The man you shot is Joe Tiller from Alaska. No record of him up there, which is unusual. I mean none at all. Tiller's car was registered to a Botree Smith from Montana, common-law wife, recently deceased. Here's where it gets interesting. Tiller's fingerprints match an Eldridge County man wanted for questioning twenty-five years ago. Virgil Caudill."

"Questioning for what?" Sanders said.

"Homicide. Victim was Billy Rodale. Back then he was top suspect in the murder of Virgil's brother, Boyd Caudill. Somebody killed Rodale. Right after that, Virgil disappeared."

"Somebody kill him, too?" Sanders said.

"The sheriff didn't think so. There's more. We got a match on the forty-five Tiller had on him. Same gun used on Leo Gowan and Linda. His fingerprints are on the gun along with the shotgun. Hack Darvis and Pete Lowe were killed at close range with the same gauge."

Mick watched the men's faces as they processed the information, assembling a narrative in their heads. He knew the questions they'd ask.

"Let me get this straight," Sanders said. "Caudill killed Rodale twenty-some years ago. Changed his name and fled to Alaska. Then last week he came here and went on some kind of rampage. Why?"

"No way of knowing," Logan said. "Maybe he's crazy. Maybe the TV told him to."

Sanders directed his glare at Mick.

"Any connection to your family?"

"Could be," Mick said. "There's more Caudills here than anybody else. Rich ones and poor ones. Town Caudills and holler Caudills. I don't know who all Linda knows. Probably a dozen."

"You just happened to kill the man who shot your sister?"

"I didn't know it was him at the time."

"Why were you onto him?"

"Like I told you," Mick said, "Johnny Boy called me. Said he'd seen the Wagoneer with no plates. He didn't know the vehicle and thought it was suspicious."

"Why didn't he do it himself?"

"He didn't say and I didn't ask."

"Following chain of command?" Sanders said. "Don't question your superior? Army protocol?"

"There wasn't anything to question. He told me about the Wagoneer and I saw it in town later. Followed it out 60 to a turnoff. I waited on the main road for a couple of hours. The Wagoneer left and I went up there."

"Why'd you wait?" Sanders said.

"Didn't know who or what was up there. I was on my own."

"Is that the army way?" Sanders said. "Being safe and careful?"

"Not hardly," Mick said. "It's my way. Hard-learned lesson."

"What'd you find?"

"Place was empty. But it looked like somebody was camping there. So I stuck around."

"Then what happened?"

"Wagoneer came back. The driver entered the house. I identified myself as deputy. He

313

pulled a gun and fired it. I shot him."

Someone tapped on the door twice. It opened and Officer Dixon came in, handed a sheet of paper to Chief Logan, and left. Logan read it and passed it to the state policeman. They both looked at Mick, who sat quietly.

"Your phone," Sanders said. "Let me see it."

"That's not necessary," Logan said.

"It's all right," Mick said. "Whatever helps."

He unlocked his phone and slid it across the table. The state policeman studied the call log, then checked the messages.

"No messages," Sanders said. "You delete them?"

"I don't text."

"Your way or the army way?"

"I don't have anybody I'm that close to," Mick said.

"What are you looking for?" Logan said.

"Sheriff Tolliver's incoming call about the Wagoneer. Came in last night. Next call is outgoing to 911. Then Hardin called you, Chet. Nothing after that."

Mick nodded, relieved. The sequence of calls would verify his timeline.

Logan tapped the paper that Officer Dixon had brought in.

"Sandra brought this over," Logan said. "It's a letter from Johnny Boy. He's requesting emergency medical leave. Has to go to Indiana. His kidney matches a cousin who was in a wreck."

"Why?" Mick said. "I thought you could get by with one kidney."

"His cousin lost one and the other is damaged. He deputized you when Linda got shot. Is that right?"

Mick nodded.

"That means you're the sheriff now," Logan said.

"I don't want it."

"If you don't take it, the mayor and judge will get together and appoint one until the next election."

"Or Linda's back on the job," Mick said.

"Yes, and you should hold onto it for her. Those politicians will stick some guy in they like. Who knows? He may keep the job."

"I can't," Mick said. "I'm under investigation."

"I think the prints and the gun put a stop to that. Caudill went on some kind of killing binge and you stopped him."

Chief Logan looked at Sanders.

"What do you think, Fred?" he said.

Sanders was staring at a framed collection of shoulder patches from various police departments. He chewed the inside of his mouth and made an expression of resigned disgust.

"Politicians suck," he said. "And yeah, they'll put their boy in. Won't be good for anybody but them. I don't like it one bit, but it's for the best."

Sanders stared at Mick as if daring him to comment. Mick understood that he was frustrated and angry.

"You'll need a deputy," Logan said. "Got anybody in mind?"

Mick nodded, watching Sanders.

"How about you, Fred?"

The long-simmering tension in the small room suddenly surged as if an explosion had sucked the oxygen away. Mick's body relaxed itself, an instinct from combat. He breathed slowly, prepared to defend himself. He was unarmed but there were objects at his disposal — a pen on the table, a lamp at hand, the coffee cup. The plastic arm from Logan's spectacles. Each option presented itself in milliseconds. He'd make the choice depending on the direction of the attack — across the table or from the side.

Sanders held Mick's gaze without blinking. His face was turning red. His eyes narrowed and Mick knew it was coming. Everything faded except the enemy. The world

316

was underwater, slowing everything but Mick. He was the swiftest fish in the sea.

A burst of laughter erupted from Sanders. It echoed off the walls and ceiling until he ran out of breath and began again. Logan joined in. Their laughter dwindled to chuckles until Logan said, "What about you, Fred?" Both men began laughing again and Mick did, too, surprised at himself. He couldn't recall the last time anything was funny. This wasn't either. It was release, the closest he could come to crying for his sister.

CHAPTER TWENTY-THREE

Mick woke at Linda's house, lying on his back, a position he'd begun in boot camp twenty years before. On the floor were his side-zip boots and the Beretta. He blinked twice, took a deep breath, and was fully awake. He rose, dressed, and boiled water for coffee. He drank it at the same table he'd eaten at as a child. He washed the cup in the same sink. Possibly it was the same water. He'd read that Earth had a finite amount of water that continued in a cycle of evaporation and rain. Maybe the coffee was made from an old bath he'd taken.

Mick's phone vibrated. It was a picture of a red tomato that he knew had bounced around Europe and the USA before landing. The image meant a second one was forthcoming from Sebastien. Within thirty seconds, the face of a fox arrived, indicating that Johnny Boy was in Corsica. Mick wondered how long he'd stay. He'd seen strong men ruined by killing and quiet men turned chatty. Others disappeared completely, like Sebastien. A small percentage managed to live a decent life and it wasn't until they were dead that people learned of their grim history. Johnny Boy's outcome was unpredictable.

Mick walked the half mile across town to Johnny Boy's place. His personal vehicle was outside, a Chrysler 200 with low mileage. If Mick hid the car it would eventually be found and raise suspicion. He could forge Johnny Boy's signature on the title and sell it out of state but would leave a trail. Getting rid of the car completely was the quickest option.

Mick drove south of town along old 1274 to Cave Run Lake. The most isolated access point was Claylick Boat Ramp, which led to a deep hole of water against the shore. Before the development, he'd swum there as a child, jumping off a steep cliff. He negotiated an overgrown dirt road to the top of the cliff and parked. He removed the VIN number strip, emptied the glove box, and rolled all the windows down. He searched the woods for a stout length of hickory. Most were brittle deadfall but he found a long branch sheared by lightning. He wedged one end against the accelerator and pressed the other end into the driver's seat. It didn't fit as well as he liked, but it only needed to work for a few seconds. He set the emergency brake and turned the key in the ignition. The engine came to life, straining against the brake like an animal on a leash. He used another stick to release the brake and watched the car leap forward as if shot from a cannon, flying off the cliff and into the lake. It bobbed twice and sank, joining the town of Yale, flooded by the dam's construction in the seventies.

Mick walked to the blacktop, called Albin the cab-driver, and requested a pickup at the boat ramp. Thirty minutes later Albin arrived, his usual cheerful self. Mick silenced him with a look, claimed to be hungover, and alluded to a romantic liaison that went awry. Albin nodded with a grin and drove to the hospital.

Juan Carlos and Raymond were in Linda's room, meaning the limit of one visitor had been lifted, a good sign. Linda was loopy from medication. J.C. cut a burrito into small chunks for her.

"What do you know, Big Bro?" Linda said. "I already heard everything from Chet and Sandra. You're the big shot hero now."

"Just till you come back."

"Or Johnny Boy," she said. "Where'd he

320

run off to? Indianapolis?"

"Muncie. It's northeast of Indianapolis."

"I don't need a damn geography lesson."

"What do you need, Sis?"

"A fucking leg that works."

"Hey," Juan Carlos said. "You cannot talk that way if you live with us. Mama Shifty doesn't like it. And I do not."

Mick glanced at Raymond, who shrugged.

"What's all this?" Mick said.

"We are taking her home to repair herself," Juan Carlos said.

"Thanks," Mick said. "Linda, do you mind if I stay at your house?"

"Fine," she said. "Take my job and my house. Heard you met a friend of mine yesterday. Fred Sanders."

"Don't tell me he's the reason you got new locks on the house."

"The very one."

"No wonder he didn't like me."

Linda chewed and swallowed a tiny piece of burrito, then sipped water from a flexible straw.

"Did Caudill say anything?" she said.

"Not a word."

"Just crazy, I guess."

Mick nodded. She lifted her hand to indicate no more food, lay her head against the pillow, and closed her eyes. Mick motioned to the door and Raymond followed. They stood in the hall and waited for a nurse to go by.

"What really happened?" Raymond said.

"Long story. Tell you later. You're going to take care of Linda?"

"Mommy and J.C. cooked it up."

"I could use a deputy."

"No."

"Just like that?" Mick said.

"I'm a food-truck operator."

"Okay, buddy. Thanks for sticking by her." Raymond dropped his chin in a brief acknowledgment. Mick told his sister he'd be back later and left. From his truck he called Sandra and asked if she knew Officer Dixon.

"I know his sister," she said. "Good family."

"Tell me about him."

"Dixon, Joseph Taulbee. Age twenty-five. Went to school for criminology. Graduated second in his class. In the Army Reserve but didn't get called up. Chet likes him."

"Sounds like you know him pretty good."

"Why, Sheriff? You getting jealous?"

"I need a deputy."

"What about Ray-Ray?"

"He already said no."

"Keep asking," she said.

"Why?"

"Between you and me, he's sick of the taco truck. He only did it to keep Juan Carlos safe. Turns out everybody likes him better than Ray-Ray."

Mick nodded and ended the call. A mile later he realized he'd neglected to say goodbye. Civilian life had its drawbacks in every direction. He wondered if his retirement was premature. No, he just needed to reacquaint himself with civilian life. Or maybe it was the other way around — the people of Eldridge County needed to get used to him.

Mick shook his head to himself. This was about Sandra, not civilians. His impulse to please women was a flaw because he was no good at it. Ten years back his wife had gotten depressed and wanted to lie on the couch all day. Mick's response had been to buy the nicest couch available — red leather with sloped armrests ideal for her head. Instead of helping, it had prolonged her depression, and now he was divorced. He shook his head again to rid himself of thought. The intensity of his focus had lifted, allowing his mind to fill with forgotten images. The red couch. His sad wife.

He wanted whiskey but needed the woods. Mick drove a looping route, using dirt road shortcuts until he reached his grandfather's land. He parked at the bottom of the hill. He climbed the way he had as a boy, slow and quiet. At the top of the hill he heard a mourning dove, early for the day. He stopped moving and watched for it. His grandfather had loved them. He'd grown millet for the doves and trained one to eat from his palm.

Mick walked past the charred cabin and entered the woods. A sense of calm immediately draped over him. He knew each tree. The birds had hushed at his entrance to the woods but their sound slowly returned, surrounding him as if in welcome. He walked unerringly to his grandfather's special spot, then a few feet away, his own. They'd often come up here to think. Sometimes together, other times alone. They never talked. It had been Papaw's greatest gift, the idea that Mick had one place where he could sit and be — his spot.

He sat against the old oak, recalling when his body was too small to span the tree. Now his shoulders stuck out on both sides. He stretched his legs. His back curved against the bark, the oak snug as an old shirt. Mick pressed his hands into the soft dirt.

He'd tampered with a crime scene and

planted evidence. He'd let four killers go free. In less than a week he'd become the worst sheriff in county history, maybe the entire state. The hills were like a slipknot — the more you struggled, the tighter they held. He realized he didn't mind. He had his spot. He closed his eyes and listened to the birds.

ACKNOWLEDGMENTS

For local history of Sharkey, Kentucky, I thank my old friends Mark Eldridge, Mona Eldridge, and Michael Campbell. I also thank a new friend, Dr. Benjamin Fitzpatrick, professor of history at Morehead State University.

For medical advice regarding gunshot wounds I'm grateful to Dr. Jean Gispen, the best doctor I've ever known. In addition I thank her four brothers, all doctors: Greg, Tom, Doug, and Steve Guyton.

For military information I thank Randy Ryan from the Eighty-Second Airborne Division.

Any and all errors are mine and mine alone.

ABOUT THE AUTHOR

Chris Offutt is the author of the novels *Shifty's Boys, The Killing Hills, Country Dark,* and *The Good Brother;* the short-story collections *Kentucky Straight* and *Out of the Woods,* and three memoirs: *The Same River Twice, No Heroes,* and *My Father, the Pornographer.* He has written screenplays for *Weeds, True Blood,* and *Treme,* and has received fellowships from the Lannan and Guggenheim foundations. He lives near Oxford, Mississippi.

The employees of Thorndike Press hope you have enjoyed this Large Print book. All our Thorndike, Wheeler, and Kennebec Large Print titles are designed for easy reading, and all our books are made to last. Other Thorndike Press Large Print books are available at your library, through selected bookstores, or directly from us.

For information about titles, please call:
(800) 223-1244

or visit our website at:
gale.com/thorndike

To share your comments, please write:

Publisher
Thorndike Press
10 Water St., Suite 310
Waterville, ME 04901